CW01024026

RUSSIAN ROULETTE

A Sixties Mystery

BERNARD KNIGHT

First published in Great Britain by Robert Hale Ltd 1968
This edition published by Accent Press 2016

ISBN 9781910939956

Copyright © Bernard Knight 1968, 2016

The right of Bernard Knight to be identified as the author
of this work has been asserted by the author in accordance
with the Copyright, Designs and Patents Act 1988.

The story contained within this book is a work of fiction.
Names and characters are the product of the author's
imagination and any resemblance to actual persons, living
or dead, is entirely coincidental.

All rights reserved. No part of this book may be
reproduced, stored in a retrieval system, or transmitted in
any form or by any means, electronic, electrostatic,
magnetic tape, mechanical, photocopying, recording or
otherwise, without the written permission of the
publishers: Accent Press Ltd, Ty Cynon House, Navigation
Park, Abercynon, CF45 4SN

To Boris, Raya, Natasha, Polina Semyonovna, and all my forensic colleagues in Moscow – with apologies to the Hotel Metropol for having a murder in their backyard!

Author's note

The Sixties Mysteries is a series of reissues of my early crime stories, the first of which was originally published in 1963. Looking back now, it is evident how criminal investigation has changed over the last half-century. Though basic police procedure is broadly the same, in these pages you will find no Crime Scene Managers or Crown Prosecution Service, no DNA, CSI, PACE, nor any of the other acronyms beloved of modern novels and television. These were the days when detectives still wore belted raincoats and trilby hats. There was no Health and Safety to plague us and the police smoked and drank tea alongside the post-mortem table!

Modern juries are now more interested in the reports of the forensic laboratory than in the diligent labours of the humble detective, though it is still the latter that solves most serious crimes. This is not to by any means belittle the enormous advances made in forensic science in recent years, but to serve as a reminder that the old murder teams did a pretty good job based simply on experience and dogged investigation.

Bernard Knight
2015

Prologue

It was one of those cold, windy Sunday nights, when torn newspapers tangled around empty milk bottles and even the tomcats cowered behind their dustbins.

Already early May, it felt like Christmas. It was even raining.

'Like sumpt'n outta goddam Dickens!' muttered the American, as he paused under a gas lamp in the Covent Garden backstreet to peer at a scrap of paper. He pushed the address back into his pocket and stared at Crouch Street with distaste.

The grimy windows of the tall grey houses scowled back at him with Victorian disdain. A row of overfilled garbage cans stood like a line of crippled pensioners along the edge of the pavement.

Glimmers of light struggled reluctantly from behind shabby curtains, but further along the street he could see a brighter glow over a doorway. Kramer shrugged his expensive overcoat higher around his neck and moved up the street until he could read the illuminated Perspex sign.

'*Happy Dragon*!' he sneered under his breath. 'What a helluva place to pick for a meeting!'

He turned in off the dismal street and began to trudge up the surprisingly well-carpeted stairway to the first floor.

In the restaurant above, Simon Smith waited with mounting impatience. He had eaten three exotic Chinese dishes, none of which he had wanted. He'd had to justify his sitting there for forty minutes beyond the arranged time. Never a lover of oriental food, his stomach was now reminding him that egg foo yung and curried prawns were incompatible. A brandy, a lager and three coffees had failed to put out the fire in his abdomen and he was beginning to wish that he had told Harry Lee Kramer to meet him in a Wimpy Bar instead of the Happy Dragon.

He looked at his watch for the second time in a minute and hissed with annoyance. His gaze strayed around the dimly lit room.

There were open tables in the central part, but all around the walls were alcoves formed by heavy brocade curtains. In these discreet niches, a few courting couples and furtive co-respondents lurked in the gloom. A slim Chinese youth glided by with empty dishes, his almond eyes flickering briefly over Simon's face.

Where the hell was Kramer? Surely even a Yank could find this place, not a hundred yards from the Strand. Simon's nerves were as good as the next man's, but after the broad hints about the nature of the proposition that Kramer had dropped on the telephone, he had every right to be a bit on edge. The delay did nothing to soothe him.

He played restlessly with his coffee cup, half-full of cold brown mud, then flicked a microscopic crumb from his lapel. A very smart, if not actually 'sharp', dresser, his normal fastidiousness was heightened by the waiting. The thirty-five guinea suit was less than half paid for and even his glassy elastic-sided shoes were not yet wholly his own. In fact, he thought sourly, unless Kramer showed up and the deal went through, his creditors would have him going around London in his underpants before the month was out.

A corner of his eye saw the swing-door open and his head jerked up in anticipation. A lean, tall figure sidled in, muffled in a tweed overcoat, which was soon spirited away by a dinner-jacketed Chinese who materialized from nowhere. After a few whispered words, the manager waved regally towards Simon's alcove.

Harry Lee Kramer came across and scowled down at the younger man.

'Say, pal, I know we're supposed to be going into the cloak-and-dagger business, but ain't this carrying it a bit far?'

Simon rose and shook hands briefly with the American, whom he had never seen before. Kramer's long, dyspeptic face turned even sourer. He slumped down into a seat opposite and began massaging his stomach with two fingers slipped between his waistcoat buttons.

'You going to eat?' asked Simon.

'Naw, I'm not having this Hong Kong chow. I had a decent steak back at the hotel … but I'll have me a drink.'

The Chinese boy appeared like the genie of the lamp. They waited in stony silence until he came back with two brandies.

Simon Smith sat primly attentive, hands folded in front of his glass, bottling up the seething fears and excitement within himself.

'Well?' he said, when he could stand Kramer's heavy silence no longer.

The American took his heavy horn-rimmed glasses off his executive-style face and began to polish the lenses with maddening slowness.

'Did you get the visa and the tickets?' he asked, ignoring Simon's question.

The other man nodded impatiently. 'They cost me every penny of that hundred quid you sent.'

Kramer ignored that as well.

'I represent a member of a big stateside corporation,' he began heavily, as if launching into an hour's lecture, 'It don't matter which one. I'm not supposed to know, so I'm sure *you're* not! '

Satisfied with his spectacles, he put them back on his nose and nudged them into place with an almost obsessive grimace.

'The research department of this outfit have had the tip-off that the Commies have developed a new kind of tool steel that's really something … I'm no engineer, God knows, just a plain old undercover man, but it seems that this stuff will slice through metal like a hot knife through butter.'

He paused to gulp some of his brandy and take a long look at his companion over the rim of the glass. *About thirty*, Kramer thought – *a bit more, perhaps*. Nicely compact, well-built shape – *make a good middleweight, though he looks too fond of his face for the ring*. Bit of a ladies' man – fair wavy hair, baby-blue eyes – *be a good conman if he had the personality to go with it*, he mused.

Simon suddenly spoke, his voice brittle with pent-up tension.

'I hope you haven't got any bloody silly ideas about me cracking safes or shinning over factory walls, have you?'

Kramer shook his head like a bull with an old sack caught in its horns.

'Naw, naw, naw … jus' let me finish, will yuh?'

He swallowed some more brandy as if it was cough mixture and winced as it hit his ulcer.

'Look, it seems that this stuff will revolutionise automated production lines – our people will be able to cut the ground from under Ford and General Motors. So they want it fast – especially before the French or the West Germans get in on the act.'

He looked around furtively and lowered his voice.

'We've already had the whisper that the Krauts have got wind of it, so we gotta beat 'em to it, see?'

Simon nodded, his eyes fixed on the other man. 'And just where do I come in – and for how much?'

Kramer peered around again, more from force of habit than from fear of being seen. He dipped a hand into his inner pocket and slid a thick envelope across the tablecloth. 'There's a thousand bucks in there. Deliver the goods – like I'm gonna tell you – and there'll be another two grand for you.'

'Pounds sterling?'

'Dollars – US.'

'I want pounds.'

'Nothing doing, bud – I got my orders. You ain't the only pebble on the beach – just the first one we happened to pick up.'

'Let's hear the details – see what it's worth.'

Harry grimaced his glasses back up his nose. 'Right … we've got another feller to do all the graft – you're just the legman. You contact this guy in Moscow and bring back a sample of the stuff for analysis.'

Simon's hand jumped from the packet as if it had suddenly become red-hot. He leant across the table. 'Bring the actual stuff back! You must be joking, chum.' He snorted. 'I thought you just wanted some bit of paper or a microdot or something … I'm not hawking a steel ingot through Soviet Customs, thank you!'

He sat back with the aggrieved air of one who has just been mortally insulted, though internally he was shaking with excitement. Kramer did another head-shaking act.

'Naw, naw, naw … there's nothing to it! What the hell, any idiot can get in and out of Russia these days, it's not like it used to be. There's nothing political in it,' he wheedled illogically, 'just a bit of good old-fashioned industrial competition, that's all.'

'Well, you get some other sucker to stick his neck out!' snapped Simon, in a rash display of falsely nonchalant heroics.

'Take it easy,' placated the American. 'We only dealt with you because it was such a cinch, even for a beginner. I know you ain't done any of this before, but with you speaking the lingo so well, it'll be a pushover. I told you, it's only legwork, no risks involved. It'll be a paid holiday!'

'I could get shot.'

'Naw, naw, naw!' Kramer made vaguely conciliatory movements with his hands.

'Or twenty years in a labour camp.'

Kramer sighed. 'How much, then?' He was never one for beating too long about the bush.

'Make those dollars into pounds.'

'You're nuts!'

There was a stirring sound across the table as Simon prepared to get up.

Harry hurriedly raised a hand. 'OK, OK ... I thought it would come to this,' he muttered, rubbing his belly mournfully. His duodenum always played him up at this point in every business deal.

Simon spoke again, his voice tremulous as fear wrestled with greed. 'And you're sure it's just a simple pick-up job?'

'Yeah, yeah ... now listen, here's what you have to do. And for Gahd's sake, don't louse it up, pal. If this contact man gets the chop, you, me and my ulcer will be outta work for a long time!'

Chapter One

An empty vodka bottle fell with a satisfying splash into the mirror-calm waters of the Baltic.

The sleek white ship slid past in the moonlight, her long wake pointing back towards the tiny flashing light that marked the Swedish coast.

The bottle had come from an open porthole on 'A' deck, which spilled light, music and a babble of voices into the quiet of the late evening. Shrill laughter and the clinking of glasses heralded yet another mid-voyage celebration.

'Of course, I thought of taking a first class cabin, but then, I said "what's the point?" … I mean, it's supposed to be a classless society, *isn't* it? … we all eat the same food, share the same decks, so why pay absolutely pounds more, just to have a private loo and an extra washbasin!'

The affected accents of the hostess battled against a transistor radio going full blast and the Assistant Purser's attempts to render 'The Foggy Dew' in his native Russian.

Simon Smith clutched the brunette's arm – a thing he did at the slightest opportunity. 'Come on, Liz, let's evaporate before the old dragon buttonholes us again.' He referred to the formidable blue-rinsed widow who was giving the party, but his companion refused to budge.

'No, not yet … I'm enjoying myself. Get me another drink, will you?'

Elizabeth Treasure spoke with the imperiousness of a beauty who is accustomed to having men trample one another to death in the rush to obey her every whim.

1

Simon meekly took her empty glass and began weaving across the cabin to the makeshift bar. His mind was churning with problems, all slightly awash in duty-free drink. Mission 'Tool Steel', as he had come to think of it, formed the backcloth of his worries but, at the moment, ways and means of overcoming Liz's stubborn resistance to his dishonourable intentions were at the forefront of his mind.

She was easily the most attractive woman on the ship, in spite of some close competition from some Swedish and Finnish girls. A chic young lady of about twenty-six, she was wonderfully dressed and exquisitely made-up. She had a figure that made Simon ache every time he looked at it. Built for conquest, her petulance and moodiness were a challenge to the amateur secret agent. He had found out very little about her in the four days since leaving Tilbury for Leningrad, except that she ran an exclusive boutique in Chelsea, along with a partner, presumably another young socialite.

Her unshakeable resistance to seduction was plaguing Simon.

He had always thought himself a pretty fast worker when it came to the love game; he had no particular pride about this – results just showed it to be a fact. Other chaps were good at golf or poker – he was good at seduction. It irked him to admit that, after four nights aboard the *Yuri Dolgorukiy*, he could get no further than some fairly advanced necking with the delectable Mrs Treasure.

As he squirmed between the last pair of shoulders in the small cabin, to arrive at the 'bar', he muttered 'It's tonight or bust!' to himself.

He rested his empty glasses on the bedside locker that was doing service as a bar.

'What will it be, old chap? Vodka and coke – vodka and gin – or vodka and vodka. Haw, haw, haw!'

Simon peered down at the flushed face of their courier, Gilbert Bynge, who was acting as barman in the intervals between nuzzling the neck of a very young and very pretty Swedish blonde.

A shambles of bottles stood on the locker and surrounding floor, most of them empty. The courier had been pitching the finished ones with carefree abandon and, so far, fortunate accuracy, through the open porthole behind him. He was now getting tipsy and it was only a matter of time before he exploded one in a shower of glass over the guests. Simon studied the remaining drinks.

'A straight vodka and one with coke … not too much coke, I'm trying to crank her up tonight.'

Gilbert Bynge leered at him and splashed vodka into the used glasses, keeping a firm grip on the blonde's waist with the other arm.

'How's the campaign going, old boy … any joy yet?'

They had discussed the problem earlier that day over beer, Gilbert being the only other man on the Trans-Europa tour who was within a decade of Simon's age.

'Not a touch yet – I'll get these drinks down and then slope off to the boat deck with her – she's a hard case.' He gathered up the glasses and set off across the cabin, leaving Gilbert to add to the line of empty bottles now floating every nautical mile across the Gulf of Bothnia.

Their overpowering hostess had thankfully not returned to Elizabeth's side, but her place had been taken by a short, rotund man with a bald head. He was gesticulating with the enthusiasm of an Arab bazaar keeper, his pink baby face gleaming with perspiration.

'Vodka and coke – that OK, Liz?'

The brunette took it with the air of someone accustomed only to the best champagne, and stitched her smile on again as she turned back to listen to Monsieur Fragonard. He appeared to be lecturing on the rival merits of Versailles and the Louvre.

Simon stood in the steaming fug, sipping his drink impatiently.

The short chappie was a Swiss merchant, voluble and boring, who latched himself on to anyone who would suffer him at any time of the day.

I'm going to draw another blank tonight if I don't get her out of this place soon, he fretted, as Fragonard jabbered on to Elizabeth.

He was distracted by some commotion in another corner, where it appeared that the Assistant Purser had fallen in a drunken stupor and shattered his head against the door. *Managing to fall full-length in this crush is an achievement in itself*, thought Simon dispassionately. The Chief Purser dragged his colleague out into the companionway and the other occupants expanded to take up the space. Almost all the twenty members of the Trans-Europa tour were there, with the exception of a few of the most senile old ladies. A couple of Soviet crewmen and some hangers-on like Gilbert's girlfriend made up the rest. Apart from Liz and the courier, not one of the tourists was under forty, and, more than once, Simon had the impression that he had joined an old folks' outing rather than an expensive continental holiday tour. Still, at the short notice that Kramer had given him, he was lucky to get into anything going Russia-wards – and Liz was a more than adequate compensation.

Jules Honore Fragonard was still gabbling away and Simon failed to catch Liz's beautiful eye. He was about to resign himself to yet another night without an attempt on her virtue, when Gilbert Bynge created a diversion by knocking the bar over.

The courier blithely stepped over the wreckage of bottles, leading his blonde by the hand.

'Booze all gone, folks!' he announced in his phoney Oxford accent. 'Let's all go to the main lounge –there's a dance on and the bar will be open for another half-hour.'

His tall, thin form loped away, the girl skipping behind him. Infected by his gaiety, the passengers, though semi-senile in Simon's view, trooped out after him in a noisy, tiddly throng.

Thankfully, the fat little Swiss man was caught up in the exodus and Simon managed to split Elizabeth away from him.

'Come on, let's get some air,' he suggested, 'Up on the boat deck for a few minutes – then we can go down to the Twist session, if you fancy it.'

Rashly, he slipped his arm around her waist.

If he wanted a response, he got it. She neatly turned out of his grasp and tucked her evening bag beneath her arm with a gesture of finality.

'This cabin has given me a headache. I'm going to turn in, Simon. Don't bother to see me down; go up in the fresh air – you look as if you need it!'

With this acid parting shot, she set off briskly for the stairs. Simon started to follow her, then subsided against the doorpost with a sigh. 'Bloody women!' he muttered with feeling. He wandered out to the deck and stared down at the racing bow wave until it made his stomach feel queasy. He *had* had a lot to drink – that vodka muck of Gilbert's was catching up with him.

'Bloody women! ' he said again and started off somewhat unsteadily for the other bar, which was at the after end of the promenade deck. It was almost empty, most passengers being either in their bunks or in the main lounge. Simon draped himself over one of the high stools as the urbane Russian barman, resplendent in most un-Marxist dinner jacket, came to serve him.

'I'll have a Three Horses, George ... no more spirits for me tonight.'

Crouched over the bottle of Dutch lager – several bottles, in fact – he moped about his troubles. The taste of

5

amorous defeat lay bitter in his mouth, but he had long-term worries as well.

'Should never have put that damn silly advert in the paper,' he growled thickly into his fourth glass of Three Horses.

The advertisement was the root of all his troubles.

Five weeks before, he had added to his rapidly mounting overdraft by inserting a paragraph in the 'Agony' columns of the *Times* and *Telegraph*.

It read *YOUNG EX-OFFICER SEEKS ANY UNUSUAL BUT HIGHLY REMUNERATIVE SERVICE. FLUENT GERMAN AND RUSSIAN. PREFER FOREIGN ASSIGNMENT, BUT ANYTHING CONSIDERED.*

'"Anything considered!",' he thought bitterly.

Of the seven replies, he had to go and pick the one that now seemed bound to get him either shot or imprisoned for life. The fact that it was the most highly paid by at least tenfold was of little consolation if he would not be around to collect.

His original idea was born out of boredom, poverty and frustration at civilian life. His eight-year commission in the regular army had left him ill-equipped for any chair-borne career. Active service in Cyprus and Malaya in an infantry battalion, but no university degree or technical qualifications, had left him high and dry when he was demobbed. A bachelor and an orphan, he had lived over-extravagantly on his gratuity for nearly two years. He failed at a variety of offbeat jobs and ended up as a second-hand car salesman. If he'd had the know-how, he might have turned to crime, as long as it was of the sophisticated 'Gentleman Jim' sort, but he had no idea where to begin.

The advertisement was the last hope. He was really looking for a military job – he rather fancied a major's rank in one of the English-officered mercenary armies that were springing up in a dozen emergent African states. But no one seemed to want another 'Mad Mike' – six of his replies consisted of four offers of Russian translation work, a post as under-manager of a stud farm in Sussex and a proposal of marriage from a lady in Tonbridge.

The translation jobs, though quite well-paid, interested him not a bit. He had learned German as a boy, living with his widowed Army father in Cologne just after the war ... the Russian came from a six-month intensive course in the Army. He had a natural flair for languages – *about the only natural ability I have, apart from womanising*, he reflected in melancholy.

The seventh, and only interesting reply, was a note, carrying no address. It stated shortly that if the advertiser would consider a small element of risk, the foreign travel could be coupled with remuneration in excess of a thousand pounds, all for only a few weeks involvement. The unsigned note gave a Mayfair telephone number which could be rung between six and eight any evening that week.

Simon had immediately dumped all the other replies in the bin and sat feverishly speculating on the offer until the hands of his watch crept around to six.

Drug smuggling? His conscience kept bobbing up against that, though the sort of money mentioned was enough to stifle most of his finer feelings. *Espionage*? No, one hardly became a spy via an advert in the *Times*.

He was little the wiser after he had made the call.

A nasal American voice introduced himself as Harry Lee Kramer and proceeded to do all the talking. Simon's name, age and background were extracted in rapid-fire questioning.

'Just want you to collect some little thing from Moscow – nothing illegal, nothing political, see ... are you interested for three grand?' He skilfully blocked all Simon's questions. 'Are you on, or not, huh?'

Simon said he was, and Kramer gave him some terse instructions, after promising to post a small advance payment for expenses. He was to get a Russian visa – took about ten days – then book a tourist trip on a round tour through Moscow. It was the start of the season and he would be able to find a vacancy easily, said Kramer.

Then they fixed up a meeting ten days or so ahead, which Simon suggested could be at the Happy Dragon.

The first pangs of doubt started at that meeting. In spite of the raised price, which in other circumstances would have sent him delirious with delight, he became progressively more apprehensive, during the day following the Happy Dragon episode.

But these regrets were nothing compared to his feelings at midnight that night.

Returning to his Bayswater serviced flatlet, he found it a shambles of overturned furniture, rifled drawers and torn cushions. That it was no ordinary burglary was only too obvious – an expensive camera, a wristwatch and a few pounds in cash were untouched.

In dismay, he sat down among the wreckage and slowly came to realize that he had just been 'done over' by someone connected with 'Operation Tool Steel'.

But *how* connected?

What was the common factor? ... his visit to the Chinese restaurant or his visa application, which had been granted that very day?

It *must* have been the Kramer meeting – thousands of people get Russian visas without having their homes turned inside out! So who was interested in his association with Kramer? Could it even be Kramer or his agents, satisfying themselves that Simon was on the level? Or the Soviets – or MI5 – or the Gehlen[1] or even the CIA?

---

[1] West German Intelligence organisation set up by US named after Reinhard Gehlen.

In the long sleepless night, his favours wavered violently between the various factions. He thought of rivals to Kramer's organization, but kept returning to the Soviets as the most likely. Influenced perhaps by a literary diet of Fleming and Deighton, he came back every time to the KGB and even SMERSH, though he had a hazy knowledge of what they actually were.

Whoever it was, he wanted no part of it. At two that morning, he had tried to telephone Kramer's number to tell him that he was opting out, but there was no reply. All through the following day, the Mayfair number remained unanswered. It seemed that the Kramer bird had flown; even the collection of the sample was to be by someone else – the American had given him a Mansion House number to ring on the thirtieth of May – the day after the Trans-Europa trip arrived home.

The next week, until the departure of the tour, was purgatory for Simon Smith. The thought of dangers unknown obsessed him. He stayed in his flat, a virtual recluse, trying to decide whether or not to abandon the scheme.

For the first day or so, he was firmly decided to pack it in – keep the money Kramer had given him and hope that the Yank wouldn't turn up to claim it.

But as the week wore on and nothing alarming happened, his natural avarice asserted itself again. The middle of the week was marked by wild swings of indecision and the consumption of a lot of whisky. Then, as departure day approached, the swings of his mental pendulum gravitated to the side of 'having a go at it'.

By the evening of departure from Liverpool Street he was resigned, if not actually determined. He decided to at least get on the boat train.

'I can always just sit tight and enjoy the trip and do nothing,' he had told himself. 'The slightest sign of trouble and Simon boy will draw back into his shell like a winkle!'

9

He consoled himself with the thought that until he actually took some step towards obtaining the tool steel, he was doing no wrong and was entitled to all the aid and other guff printed on the inside of his passport.

So, on the fateful twelfth of May, he was installed in the Tilbury boat train, nattily decked out in an expensive sports suit, a legacy of the days when his gratuity was intact. His nylon case was in the rack above and sitting there with three inches of patterned sock exposed above his suede shoes, he looked more an off-duty executive than a tremulous spy off on his first assignment.

Though he would not have admitted it to himself, he rather enjoyed the mental image. A young, suave, good-looking chap, lolling nonchalantly in a first-class compartment, unsuccessfully trying to do the *Telegraph* crossword ... but *really* secret agent Simon '008' Smith!

In every man there is a little James Bond trying to get out, and as long as Simon was able to keep his mind on the pseudo-glamour and push the hideous risk of reality to the background, he was able to enjoy himself.

Much of this churned through his mind as he sat hunched over the bar in the Russian vessel. He was getting more and more fuddled. His capacity for beer after eight years in an officers' mess was enormous, but the unfamiliar vodka earlier on had lost him his grip on sobriety.

Nothing further had happened to resurrect his fears about 'the job', but the Liz Treasure episode tonight needed drowning in drink. She had first crossed his line of sight when getting off the train at Tilbury. He had at once recognized an unusually attractive prospect and with his practised adroitness, had managed to stumble over her cases on the platform.

With profound, but not overdone, apologies he had contrived to help her through the Customs and onto the ship. Years of experience had taught him not to push things too fast at that stage, but from then on he had manipulated for their paths to cross with great frequency. Though he couldn't manage the same table in the dining room, by the first evening he was buying her a drink in the bar.

For the first two days, things went with a swing, but then stuck when they were becoming most interesting. Though she was one of the most luscious women he had ever known, he soon realized that she either had a thick streak of ice down the middle or had an armour-plated lining to her velvety skin.

From the first, his intentions were entirely dishonourable, but she was able to guard her virtue with a ruthlessness and efficiency that he had never encountered before.

Normally, she did this with a deftness that caused no offence and merely invited him to come back for another try; but she had moods of petulance, and tonight he had been given the brush-off in no uncertain terms.

'Must have been the liquor on my damned breath,' he grunted, perversely beckoning George to bring him another bottle.

He began to drink with aggressive enthusiasm, but before he was halfway through, another member of the tour lurched into the bar and sat heavily on the next stool. Simon's grade of intoxication became a pale shadow compared to his neighbour's, though Michael Shaw carried it with the ease of long practice.

He was by no means a sociable drinker, and their common bond of drunkenness brought no more conversation than a mumbled 'Hello there'.

Shaw ordered a double whisky from the smooth barman and when he received it, he subsided into a heavy-breathing reverie, the only outward signs of his bad state being the tremor of his hands and the way his feet kept slipping off the chromium rail beneath his stool.

Simon tried a few rather slurred openings about the weather, the recent party and the prospects of a good holiday, but was met with such a vague and sullen response that he soon gave up. As he finished his drink, he covertly watched the big Irishman from behind the hand that supported his own chin on the bar. Michael Shaw must have been an inch or so above six feet and had shoulders and limbs to go with it. He seemed to be a great athlete badly gone to seed. His eyes were watery and red-rimmed and he was growing a flabby paunch beneath the shapeless sports jacket.

A newcomer to the tour, he had only joined the ship that day, at the Stockholm port of call. Gilbert had mentioned casually that he was expecting a late arrival … and that the newcomer would be a journalist from Dublin, extending his Swedish holiday. *From the looks of Shaw now*, thought Simon, *a holiday in Russia would be a waste of money* – any bar in the world would have satisfied his wants, without him trailing around Europe.

Shaw's foot slipped again and his chin, cupped in a ham-like hand, jerked down as his elbow slithered off the edge of the bar.

Simon heard him curse under his breath – then the bearded Irishman suddenly turned to him. 'No particular offence, mister, but after seeing the mob on this tour, I just had to be getting myself well-plastered tonight.'

Simon grinned a little too widely and got his apparently enlarged tongue into motion. 'Don't worry about my feelings … I've got the same bellyache myself – like an outing from a Darby and Joan club, isn't it!'

There was a long silence, while Shaw gulped the rest of his drink and silently gestured the barman to pour another. He made no move to offer one to Simon.

He decided to speak again. 'I was desperate enough to leave Stockholm – but if I'd known it was going to be like

12

this, I'd have trailed back to Cork – there's more life in any street corner pub there than the whole of the Baltic put together.'

This speech seemed to exhaust his conversational powers. Simon tried a few more openers, but was received by grunts only.

The deep-set brown eyes of the Irishman stared fixedly down at his glass from under the fringe of tangled red hair. Most of his leonine head was covered with red hair of some sort – the untidy beard, wild moustache and overlong hair, which covered his crumpled collar like a mane.

Simon finished his drink and walked with exaggerated steadiness to the door, where he spoilt the effect by tripping over the step. His cabin was on B Deck, Number 45, being up on the port side towards the bow.

He negotiated the steep stairs and narrow companionways with some difficulty, still sober enough to be thankful that the passages were deserted, so that no one could see him banging into the bulkheads. He soon got confused as to his whereabouts. He hazily remembered that his cabin was next to a bathroom and that an illuminated green sign stuck out from above the door. Thankfully, he came across the sign quite easily and groped his way groggily to the adjacent door. Turning the handle, he staggered inside.

The light was on, but he was in no condition to remember whether he had left the switch down when he left.

Then he looked around at the unmade bed, the clothes draped over the backs of chairs and the littered magazines on the floor.

'Damn ... wrong room. Mus' be the wrong bloody deck!'

He stepped out and shut the door, convinced that he had come down too many stairs, to C Deck. Then his bleary eyes looked again at the outside of the door and got the silver numbers into focus.

'Forty – five! God, it *is* mine!' Fear fought the alcohol, and won. He jerked the door open again and stood swaying in the entrance, looking once more at the disordered cabin.

No doubt about it … he had been 'worked over' yet again!

Chapter Two

Simon Smith sat dejectedly in a quayside cafe, watching the rain beat down on Helsinki.

The *Yuri Dolgorukiy* was berthed a quarter of a mile away and the passengers had a few hours to wander ashore on the last stop before Russia.

He had tried to persuade Elizabeth Treasure to come with him after lunch, but she was still in a distant mood, pleading a headache. Just as he was leaving, she relented a little. She said she might meet him, if she felt better, on the town quay at two thirty.

It was now twenty past three, and there was no sign of her. He had wandered from the ship across a small bridge that connected the island where the *Yuri* lay, to the mainland and reached the broad quayside where an open market was just closing up.

He had ambled between the stalls of potted plants and vegetables for a while, then stared over the wharf at the bargaining of the fishermen in their little boats with the local housewives.

It started to drizzle just after two. He carried on up the street from the quay, stopping to buy yesterday's *Express* at a newsagent's. The rain came down more heavily and he had no mackintosh. After sheltering for a dismal fifteen minutes in a tram shelter, he made a dash for a small cafe on the quayside, from where he could keep a lookout for the lovely Mrs Treasure. The time went by and he still sat at a table in the window, drinking hot coffee with the steam gently rising from both his cup and his damp shoulders.

He glowered through the rain-spotted window, cursing everything in general, and Liz and Kramer in particular.

There was no sign of her on the cobbled quay – it was deserted except for a mechanical sweeper sloshing up the market debris.

He pulled the English paper from his side pocket, swearing again as the sodden pages pulped in his hand.

He skimmed through the headlines about some new facet of the economic crisis, then idly went through the smaller items lower down the page. He read one without comprehension – then his heart seemed to bound into his throat and in desperate haste, he devoured the paragraph again.

YARD MAN JOINS HUNT FOR BERKSHIRE KILLER

Detective Superintendent Gordon Young, of Scotland Yard's Murder Squad, yesterday travelled to Abingdon to assist the Berkshire police in their hunt for the killer of American business executive Harry Lee Kramer, who was found shot on Tuesday night. The discovery of his body in a ditch on a lonely country road was fully reported in yesterday's Express As Mr Kramer was known to have been living in London until a few days ago, a police spokesman said it is possible that the body was 'dumped' in the countryside.

Simon's mind shut down for a moment or two – he was incapable of coherent thinking, so great was the shock. Then he recovered enough to re-read the item again, as if by some magic it would prove to be some awful optical illusion.

But the harsh black print remained on the damp paper in all its fearfulness. Kramer was dead – murdered!

While the rain beat down outside and his coffee grew cold inside, he sat feverishly trying work out the significance of the news. Was this connected with 'Tool Steel'? Kramer was a professional agent – he must have had a finger in a dozen pies. This murder need be nothing to do with the present affair – but *was* it, nevertheless? Simon had no particular emotions about the actual killing. He had met Kramer for only a few moments and, whilst he wished him no ill, his main interest in the tragedy was for his own skin.

This, together with last night's ransacking of his cabin, was too much.

'What in God's name are you doing here?' he asked himself fiercely. 'You could still be flogging second-hand Cortinas at thirty quid a week – not sitting here waiting for a knife in your back or a row of Russian bullet holes across your chest!'

His fingers trembled as he picked up his cup. He drank without noticing that it was cold, and called for another. The first shock of last night's discovery had passed, but now it had been replaced with something worse.

Several times since breakfast, he had decided to call the whole thing off and catch a plane from Helsinki back to London. Now the temptation was even stronger.

He could hardly tell what stopped him getting a taxi back to the ship to pick up his cases and then going off to the airport – it would be so easy; it would be Kramer's money he would travel on. So easy – the sensible, logical thing to do – cut one's losses and clear out before the shooting started!

Simon's fair head drooped as he rested his elbows on the table and ran fingers through his hair in an agony of indecision. He had a little over three hours in which to make up his mind – the ship sailed at seven o'clock.

Indecision was always a torment to him – again his natural avarice for the extra couple of thousand fought against the possible risks. Yet he had a strong, almost unrecognized streak of obstinacy in him. How did he know that there was much risk? Kramer's death might well be nothing at all to do with this affair – and no one had yet died of having their room searched.

He got up abruptly and went out – the rain was easing now and there was no sign of Liz; not that he expected her now, it was getting on for four o'clock.

He stood indecisively for a moment, then turned left along a road at right angles to the quay, leading to the city centre. His feet were still trying to lead him to the nearest airline office, though his brain had vetoed the idea.

After a few yards, his brain won the battle.

'To hell with them!' he said loudly, to the surprise of three pigeons and one old man.

He turned sharp right into a side street that ran behind, and parallel to, the imposing façade of the quayside buildings. He walked briskly, as if afraid that his feet might betray his new-found purpose in going back to the ship.

A few more yards brought him to the quiet cathedral square, but he had no eyes for the domed basilica at the top of a great flight of steps, or the sedate government buildings that lined the square. He kept his eyes on a small street right opposite. Hunched down against the wet breeze, he hurried on.

It was obvious that if he kept straight ahead, he would come to the waterfront which joined the main quay at right angles, the bridge to the *Dolgorukiy*'s berth being at the junction.

Crossing the square, he plunged down a narrow street lined with tall grey warehouses. It was on a slope and at the bottom he glimpsed open water.

A large truck was manoeuvring out of a gateway and he had to stop while it got into the narrow street.

As he stood waiting, a raincoated figure fifty yards behind him stepped nimbly into a doorway.

The truck grumbled its way down the alley and Simon carried on to the main road at the bottom, which ran along the water's edge. The rain started to come down heavily again. He pulled up his jacket collar in a useless effort and hurried along the deserted road towards the bridge, now dimly seen through the sweeping rain. A few cars swished by and then he was alone – so he thought.

The road had no proper sea wall like the main quay, just a muddy slope, on which were a few beached boats and some small repair yards. The rain began to come down in torrents and he looked for somewhere to shelter. The water was dripping from his eyebrows, half-blinding him, but he could see a crude corrugated iron boat shelter a few yards off the road.

He hurried to it across the sodden grass and dived in thankfully. A wooden fishing boat was propped up inside but no one was in it. The rain beat a deafening tattoo on the tin roof and he had no way of hearing the cautious footsteps squelching up behind him.

He stood with his back to the open end of the shed, idly looking at the boat.

There was a sudden sucking of rubber soles in the mud as the intruder leapt, but Simon had no time to turn.

Fingers closed like a vice around his neck and nails dug into his windpipe. He almost died there and then, out of sheer terror, but clung to consciousness long enough to realize that someone was killing him.

His vision went red, then black – before he collapsed in a head-bursting climax of asphyxia.

Kyrill Pokrovsky, the Chief Purser, and First Officer Yutkevich waited restlessly at the head of the gangway.

The purser looked at his wristwatch about twice every minute, while the other leaned over the rail to peer endlessly through the drizzle at the roadway behind the quayside warehouse.

'Ten minutes to sailing time!' fretted Yutkevich. He put his head down over the ropes of the gangway platform and called down to a uniformed Finnish dock official, who stood on the wharf below.

'Any news of them?'

The Finn shrugged and waved towards the office set in the end of the warehouse.

'They try the hospitals now!' he shouted.

A telephone tinkled inside the hull of the *Yuri Dolgorukiy* and the First Officer stepped inside the oval steel door to answer it.

'Yutkevich – *da, tovarishch*[2] captain, we have tried that … yes, telephoned twice … yes, captain.'

He hung the instrument up on the wall of the carpeted foyer and stood staring for a moment at the oil painting of a medieval horseman from whom the ship took its name. His mind was on the captain … he was thinking that he, Yutkevich, should have been giving the orders.

Twenty years with the Morflot fleet and still only a First Officer, while a dozen younger men had gone to the top over him. He snorted and put the bitterness behind him for a moment to concentrate on the problems of the present. He walked back on to the top of the gangway. 'Blast all British tourists!' he growled to Pokrovsky, 'Especially those who don't come back when they should.'

Unlike the purser, he found it a continual strain to be polite to Western tourists.

The ship was due to sail from Helsinki dead on nineteen hundred hours and all passengers were supposed to be aboard one hour before this. Today, most of them had returned early because of the rain, but two had failed to show up – Mr Simon Smith and Mrs Elizabeth Treasure.

The news had spread rapidly through the passengers in the usual manner of all happenings aboard ship and a line of curious faces peered over the rails.

After a few moments, Yutkevich gave a final glance at his watch, then craned his neck upwards at the midshipman who controlled the winch that pulled up the

---

[2]Comrade

gangway. 'Stand by. We sail in three minutes, whether they come or not!'

He turned to Pokrovsky, still standing alongside him. 'The comrade captain says we sail on schedule. If these idiots want to lose the rest of their holiday, then they're welcome. No doubt they can raise the price of another ticket from their speculations.'

The purser said nothing. The other man was a dry, humourless fellow but, as he was the ship's political representative, it did no one any good to antagonise him. His rigid dialectics, together with his bitterness at being repeatedly being passed over for promotion, had soured him beyond redemption.

The purser was jerked out of his ruminations by the sound of heavy boots rattling on the wharf. A junior immigration officer ran up to the Finnish official on the edge of the quay. They spoke rapidly together, then the older one hurried up the ramp to the Russian officers. He spoke no Russian and they no Finnish, so, as often happened, English rather incongruously became the lingua franca.

'Telephone from one of the city police stations – they have these English people there. The woman is not sick, but something has happened to the man Smith. They are bringing them to the ship now.'

Yutkevich jumped to the telephone to call the bridge, while Pokrovsky tried to find out more information. 'What's wrong with this man – if he has some serious disease, we cannot have him back on board.'

The Finn shrugged. 'I do not know – I think he was picked from the water.'

To save him further talk, a blaring 'hee-haw' of a motor siren sounded in the distance and within seconds, a cream Volvo ambulance rushed in through the gates alongside the warehouse. It pulled up near the gangway and under the avid eyes of the drama-starved passengers, two attendants got out and opened up the doors at the back.

A pale Elizabeth Treasure was helped down first, to stand by while the ambulance men expertly slid out a stretcher. On it was the even paler faced Simon Smith, muffled up to the chin with a grey blanket.

Before the men could start taking the stretcher up the gangway, there was a commotion on the platform and the captain of the *Yuri* strode out.

He was something of a mystery figure to the tourists; hardly any had set eyes on him before. Fairly young, tall and good-looking, he had a serious set to his jaw that explained how he got the command of seven million roubles-worth of new ship, whilst older men like Yutkevich remained First Officers.

'Stop those men,' he rapped out in Russian. Yutkevich ran down the gangway at the double. On political matters, he might be able to tell the captain a thing or two, but, when it came to the running of the ship, if the Old Man said 'Jump!', everyone jumped. The stretcher was slid back into the Volvo and everyone on the quayside stood and waited. Then the more familiar figure of the ship's doctor appeared and together with Yutkevich, went down to the ambulance.

The surgeon climbed into the back, while the First Officer had an animated conversation with Liz Treasure.

After crouching over the stretcher for a moment or two, the doctor came out and climbed back to the gangway platform where the captain had stood impassively all the while.

There was another rapid discussion, then the captain vanished into the ship. The doctor waved a beckoning hand at the quayside and the stretcher was pulled out again. A slow procession climbed the gangway to the accompaniment of a long blast on the ship's siren.

Ten minutes later, the *Yuri Dolgorukiy* was starting to thread her way between the islands lying off Helsinki harbour. By that time, Simon Smith was bedded down in the sickbay of the vessel. Elizabeth Treasure was having another interview with the doctor and first officer – it was necessary to find out what had happened, for entry in the ship's log, explained Yutkevich.

She sat in the purser's room behind the counter in the ship's foyer to tell her story. Her normal haughty veneer was badly cracked and she sat nervously twisting her handkerchief as she spoke.

'I was supposed to have met Mr Smith on the main quay in Helsinki at two thirty – I felt unwell, and only decided to go much later – so as not to disappoint him,' she added with a trace of her usual condescension.

'He wasn't there and, as it began to rain heavily again, I started back. As I came over that little bridge ...' she fluttered a hand vaguely in the direction of Finland, '... I saw a little crowd gathered and naturally went to look. Under the bridge supports, a couple of men were pulling something out of the water – it was a man's body. I thought he had drowned. They started to give him artificial respiration when they got him to the bank, then began shouting – he was obviously alive. I went a little nearer and was shocked to find that it was Simon ... Mr Smith!'

Yutkevich looked at her large brown eyes, the jet-black lashes looking almost stark against the pallor of her face, which even make-up could not disguise.

'Did anyone tell you how he came to be in the water?'

'No one seemed to speak English, until a policeman came up. He spoke it well and sent someone to phone for an ambulance, but a police van came along first and they put him in that.'

'What about Mr. Smith – did he recover quickly?'

'Oh yes – he suddenly coughed and struggled to sit up – he could hardly speak, though – still can't, in fact.'

'He has said nothing about what happened?'

'No – not to me. The policeman told me that his head had been caught on one of the bridge supports at water level, holding his chin above water – that saved him from being drowned.'

Yutkevich wrote everything down in a notebook and then she was courteously led back to her cabin by a stewardess who offered to stay with her if she was needed.

The two officers made their way to the captain's cabin, where the ship's doctor was already waiting. He had just come from examining Simon Smith in the sickbay.

After a short, very serious conference, the radio officer was sent for and he soon was hurrying back to his transmitter, clutching an urgent message for Leningrad Marine Radio.

The captain, Pokrovsky, and Yutkevich then made their way as unobtrusively as possible to cabin forty-five. For the third time, his belongings were searched, but this time in a tidy, methodical manner. All his cases were opened, the drawers and cupboards checked in an amateur, but efficient way.

Pokrovsky removed the mattress from the vacant upper bunk and Yutkevich started on the one below, while the captain watched.

'Ahhh!' … a triumphant bellow came from the politically minded First Officer. He had found proof indeed of the rascally intentions of the capitalist infiltrators!

The others pushed forward to look as he dragged the mattress further off the bunk. There, nestling against the bulkhead, was a small black automatic pistol.

Ten minutes later, the radio was rattling out another urgent signal to Leningrad Marine.

Chapter Three

Detective Captain Alexei Pudovkin shrank deeper into the armchair and glared balefully at his stockinged feet. He concentrated on a small hole developing over his left big toe and, using this as a Yoga focus, tried hard to blot out his immediate surroundings.

It was useless. He had already tried putting his fingers in his ears, but the sound still came through. He had even used a trick remembered from his childhood –making a deep humming noise and holding his nose to force the sound up to his ears. This might have been proof against midnight house noises fifty years ago in Minsk, but as a defence against Darya's shrill nagging, it was a miserable failure.

She came to the door of the living room now, wiping her reddened hands on her apron as if practising manual strangulation.

'… and why is it that you work later than Savitsky almost every night, eh? *He* can get home to take his wife to the stadium or the cinema a couple of times a week … you're senior to him, but you have to stay at that old Petrovka all hours!'

Alexei had given up God to join the Party, but now he found great relief in a muttered blasphemy.

Darya Pudovkina vanished back into her kitchen, to bang pots around with needless violence. Alexei sighed and groped a hand over the arm of the chair, feeling for his bottle of beer. As he poured the remains into his glass, he thought wistfully of the glorious decade before his second marriage.

A rapid rise from superfluous detective officer to captain in the Moscow Militia and the freedom of bachelorhood – or more precisely, widowerhood – were a delight to the memory.

Now all he had was Darya and the weariness of advancing age. Even the police force seemed monotonous these days – he wondered what had happened to all his old enthusiasm and ambitions. He would never rise to major now – even crime and its detection seemed dull – or was it just the creeping mental paralysis of approaching senility?

He drank some more beer and tried to drown the distant tirade from the kitchen with reminiscences ... that murder in Sokolniki Park, that was a good one. The bomb scare in the Byelorusskiy Voczal railway station ... and oh, that year's secondment to Hungary in fifty-eight, that was the high spot.

His wife's voice crashed into his daydreams like a tank hitting a brick wall. A rolled-up string bag struck him on the side of the head.

'Here, take that and get off your backside down to the store!'

Alexei hauled himself to his feet, swearing, but softly enough not to be heard.

'... and leave those socks for me to mend tonight. What will all the other wives think when they hear that their husband's Division Captain goes around like a gypsy!'

He finished his beer, shuffled his feet into his shoes and pulled on his blue uniform jacket.

Darya appeared in the doorway like a puppet on strings. 'Get a bottle of sour cream and some nice sweet wine – you know my sister likes it! Last time she was here you deliberately got that sour Kazakh stuff to annoy me ...so mind you get Georgian tonight!'

Pudovkin nodded his long head dismally and trudged silently to the other door leading into the corridor. He had learned that it was useless to argue when she got on to the inevitable subject of her family.

He let himself out and shut the door with relief. Even a trip down to the shop was welcome – part of the reason that he spent so much extra time in the Petrovka Street Headquarters was that he far preferred it to his own apartment.

Alexei ambled towards the lift, wondering if he was too old at fifty-three to apply for another secondment. *Hungary is too near*, he thought – Vladivostok was probably the nearest place out of earshot of Darya's tongue!

The lift clattered to a stop four floors below and all his urgings on the button failed to bring it any higher. With a sigh, he began to walk down the stairs – the faulty lift reminded him of yet another of his wife's grouses: '… and why can't we live in a *new* apartment block like the other senior officers? Making me live in this half-derelict old section house just because you've been here for years, yak, yak …!'

As his feet echoed down the bare concrete stairs, he noticed, as if for the first time, the peeling paint on the walls and the rude words pencilled by the children. It *was* a dump, he had to admit, but it had been home to him ever since he came back from the war. Their actual apartment was as comfortable as he could wish – there was plenty of money to buy everything except space. He sometimes thought that Darya was secretly annoyed that his pay was so good; it deprived her of the chance to nag him about being mean. With no children and her own job as a cashier in a Gorky Street store, they could afford almost anything. Already this year they'd had a new television and an elaborate radiogram. She'd even been hinting about a car these past few months … he could *just* afford a little Moskvich but, thank God, there was no garage space.

These ramblings brought him down to the ground floor. He pushed through a crowd of chattering children and parked bicycles in the entrance hall and came blinking into the afternoon sun of a bright spring day.

Looking up at the great yellow block that housed hundreds of policemen and their families, he grumbled, 'What the devil does she want to move for?', then trudged along the pavement towards the store. The major part of the ground floor was given over to a branch of Number Fifty-five Store, which supplied almost all the shopping needs of the surrounding flats. Alexei Pudovkin pushed his way through the crowded food store and bought the cream, the wine, and some beer for himself. Stuffing them into the string bag, the badge of the true Moscow suburbanite, he made his way out, going as slowly as he could.

'Hi, Alexei Alexandrovich, going on the booze again?' a cheerful voice hailed him from behind.

'Vasily! I thought you were on extra duties – that assault job.'

'All finished! He gave himself up at two o'clock – walked into Petrovka crying like a baby. He won't bother any more women for the next twenty years, at least.'

Vasily Moiseyenko, a detective lieutenant and one of Pudovkin's assistants, hoisted himself perkily on to a nearby window sill and sat swinging his legs while he rolled a cigarette. A round-faced, curly-haired young man, he looked utterly unlike a militia officer. Dressed in his off-duty sports shirt and grey slacks, Alexei thought he looked more like a professional footballer.

'You look as miserable as hell, captain,' said Vasily cheerfully. Pudovkin nodded glumly. He knew he should act like his colleagues Ivkov and Shebalin and discourage the junior man's easy familiarity, but he was glad of a bit of companionship after the freeze-up in the sixth-floor apartment.

He realized that Vasily thought a lot of him, too. Alexei provided a father-figure for him – the younger man's parents had both been killed in the Great Patriotic War and Alexei's only son from his first marriage had died in the bombing of Smolensk. So each of them knew, without ever saying anything, that each owed and gave the other something.

The detective captain put his chinking bag on the window ledge and leaned against the wall, basking in the May sunshine.

'Darya's like a forest bear with the bellyache today – her blasted sister and brother-in-law are coming again tonight.'

'The one with the warts? Let's hope we have a multiple murder, so you can get called away.'

'Ay, it would be a mercy. She's cooking enough food up there to feed the whole of our Number One Precinct.'

Vasily cocked a knowing eye at his chief. He had learned to read his moods like a book and he could see that things were even worse than usual. Over the last year, since his operation for a duodenal ulcer, Pudovkin's face had got lined and pinched, his stubbly hair was now grey all over and he was so thin and stooped that his blue uniform hung on him like rags. Over the last few months, Vasily had seen him slow up and withdraw into himself – he seemed to live mainly in the past.

'I'd better get back up there.' Alexei picked up his bottles, but made no attempt to move. He stared across the street to where the greenness of Gorky Park could be seen between two tall buildings. The masts of a ship on the Moskva river slid past in the middle distance.

'Reminds me of the Danube at Budapest, Vasily Sergeivich ... remember it?'

Moiseyenko laughed and jumped down from the window sill. 'Don't I just – the best months of my life, so far. You had a whole year of it, you lucky dog. That was *real* police work, *real* living – not stolen bicycles, drunken rapes and *stilyagi*[3] fights on a Sunday night!'

A woman walked past, her strident voice accusing her small son of something. Alexei started and the image of his wife forced Hungary from his mind.

'Must be going, Vasily, or she'll chew my ear off –the damned tribe of relatives will be here before long.'

'Right, comrade captain!' Moiseyenko threw him a mock salute. 'See you in the morning – let's hope for something good for a change. It's been dead lately, apart from last night's job ... though, of course, low crime rates *are* good for the progress of the State,' he added with a guilty afterthought proper for a young Party member.

Alexei grinned at the boy's earnestness –a rare smile on that leathery face.

'Perhaps it's the quiet before the storm, Vasily Sergeivich,' he said. If he had remembered his idle comment the next morning, he might have thought himself to have the gift of second sight.

'Where are they now?' demanded the fat man behind the desk.

Alexei Pudovkin looked at the clock on the wall of the Commissioner's office. 'It's ten to eleven now – they'll be landing at Sheremetyevo just after noon.'

The Colonel of Militia wriggled a finger in his ear, a habit that indicated deep thought, but one which had revolted Alexei for years.

'We'd better watch them right from the start,' he muttered. 'Though what in hell we're supposed to be looking for, I don't know!'

---

[3]Delinquent teenage rock-and-roll-loving children of affluent parents.

His protuberant eyes peered petulantly at the detective captain, as if it was Pudovkin's fault that the case had been thrust on them.

Alexei pointed at the telegram from Leningrad that he had received half an hour earlier.

'I know that man Ilyichev … met him at the Detectives' school one year. He's good, wouldn't waste our time.

Commissioner Igor Mitin heaved his vast bulk from his chair and waddled to the window. In spite of his ugliness, his bad temper and his endless complaining, he too was a good policeman.

'Better ring this Ilyichev, Alexei Alexandrovich – get some more details.'

'He says in his wire that he's sending them on.'

'I want to know now!' barked Mitin, his close-cropped head creaking around on his elephantine neck. 'I want to know what we're supposed to be watching … is it a pickpocket or an assassin?'

Pudovkin's thin, weary face lit up briefly. 'Let's hope it's an assassin!'

The commissioner glowered at him.

'Always after the excitement, *tovarishch*. You should have transferred to Uzbekistan and chased bandits!'

He turned back to the window and scowled down on Petrovka Street. It was busy with speeding trucks and cars, many of them police vehicles coming and going from this building; Number 38, the Militia Headquarters of the Moscow City Soviet.

'Take a car and go out yourself, Alexei – we'd better start this thing the right way, if you keep harping on about how good they are in Leningrad.'

Pudovkin grinned. There was always this pantomime between them, both grown old in the militia. Mitin would grouse and moan, but give every assistance and no interference, whilst Alexei would be the humble, servile assistant until the door shut behind him, when he did just as he pleased.

As the cadaveric detective made for the door, Colonel Mitin banged his desk. 'Take this message form and start a file – let's hope it's going to be a thin one … and take a man with you to the airport – you're too old to go

on your own – the sooner you retire the better!'

Pudovkin shut the door on this parting shot and hurried to his own office on the floor below. As senior duty officer that morning, he'd had the telegram brought to him for action, but it seemed so unusual that he felt obliged to refer it to the commissioner of the Detective Department.

The message was very terse and gained in urgency by its brevity –*DTO 09008567 LENINGRAD CENTRAL REQUEST CLOSE SURVEILLANCE ENGLISH TOURIST PARTY TRANSIT MOSCOW HOTEL METROPOL BY AEROFLOT FLIGHT 142 ETA 1205. PARTICULAR INTEREST SIMON SMITH VISA DZ14564 NO OFFENCE YET. WAS ARMED. FURTHER DETAILS FOLLOWING. ILYICHEV.*

As an example of tantalising obscurity, it was a masterpiece.

Alexei reached his small office, a partitioned corner of the main CID room on the first floor of Petrovka. He squeezed himself behind the filing cabinets to sit at his desk, which was a regulation size smaller than Mitin's.

After booking a call to Leningrad on the militia line, he read and re-read the telegram, as if hoping to find additional information hidden between the lines. The telephone clicked and rattled as it bridged the hundreds of miles between the two cities, while Pudovkin scowled down at the crumpled paper, elated and yet almost fearful of hoping for too much to come of it.

'Surveillance?' he repeated between his teeth.

A particularly loud click deafened him and he hastily put the receiver to his other ear. He slid a hand over the mouthpiece and roared at the top of his voice 'Moiseyenko, come here!'

Within seconds, Vasily put his head around the door. His desk was almost outside Alexei's door and the older man's lung power, deceptively strong and deep for such a scrawny body, acted as their 'intercom'.

He waved the message at the lieutenant. 'Start a new file – and ring the transport pool. We're going to Sheremetyevo in a few minutes.'

He waved the younger man away as the switchboard at last connected him with Leningrad Militia HQ.

Pudovkin listened a great deal and spoke sparingly, his pen flying over a notepad on his desk.

'Thanks, Ilyichev, I'll let you know how things develop.'

He hung up and stared at his scribbling pad. He was even more perplexed than before, but at least he knew a little more background.

A few moments later, he was being driven by Vasily Moiseyenko northwards through Moscow, towards one of the four airports that served the capital.

'I've opened a file and put Zhdanov on to checking the passport and visa end of it,' reported the lieutenant. 'I rang the Ministry of the Interior, but they'll take all day to look things up. Didn't have time to contact Intourist, but Zhdanov can do that as well.'

He swung the black Volga expertly into the mid-morning traffic of the Sadovaja-Karetnaya, part of the old circular road that used to mark the limits of Tsarist Moscow.

'We'll have to step on it to get to Sheremetyevo by the time the plane lands.'

He trod on the accelerator with glee. Pudovkin grunted. He sat hunched in the front passenger seat, looking like some scrawny old eagle, with his hollow cheeks and hooked nose. The coat he wore was black and shapeless; if

Darya hadn't complained about it so much, he'd have thrown it out, but now he hung on to it out of sheer cussedness. Today he was wearing it over his uniform, as a screen against curious eyes at the airport. Unlike foreign police forces, the Soviet detectives were not allowed to wear plain clothes – that kind of work was supposed to be left to either the Public Prosecutor's department or to the political police, the KGB Yet it was sometimes advisable to be discreet, and the regulations could be stretched in a remarkable elastic manner. Moiseyenko had his plastic raincoat, so if they both left their blue caps in the car, they would pass as civilians at a distance.

Vasily turned again, this time up into Kalyayevskaya Street and tore past a string of heavy trucks, their green tailboards with the foot-high registration letters crawling along to annoy any driver in a hurry The speedometer needle crept well above the town limit as they passed the stadium and the railway station in Butyrskaya Street, then they flashed under a flyover and were on the derestricted motorway of the Dmitrovskaya Highway leading northwards out of the capital.

'Don't go and kill us just before the best case we've had this month, young fellow,' grunted Alexei, as the Volga ripped past the other traffic.

'Safe as the Kremlin, boss … what's the drill when we get there?'

'No idea … our Fat Father upstairs told me to watch and observe, whatever that might mean.'

The suburbs of Moscow sped by, then some industrial estates, but soon they were in open country, the famous 'green belt' around Moscow. Moiseyenko slowed down after a few kilometres and took a left-hand turn off the highway into a secondary road winding through the birch woods.

Soon the whistle of jets and the rumble of piston engines heralded the airport. The car came out of the trees and they found themselves driving along the perimeter wire of Sheremetyevo.

Alexei Pudovkin seemed to rise up out of his shabby overcoat. *His neck came out like a tortoise*, thought Vasily, looking from the corner of his eye. The senior militiaman suddenly seemed to radiate alertness. Vasily had noticed this before, on a job. The apathetic slouch went and the captain's eyes seemed to get harder and brighter.

He began snapping orders as he surveyed the geography of the airport buildings. 'Park well away from the terminal – over there will do.'

Vasily drew up in a corner of the car park, the militia car hidden behind a fire tender.

They walked over to the old terminal building, which was still being used for internal flight arrivals, the international terminal gleaming in the sunlight across the main runway. The whine of a nearby Ilyushin made conversation impossible until the doors of the terminal swung behind them. A bored official behind the reception desk told them that the Leningrad plane was due in at that moment and, sure enough, the whistle of great engines almost drowned his last words.

An Aeroflot TU-104 flashed down the runway and taxied back up to the terminal. It came at a screaming crawl almost up to the windows of the lounge and swung around to stop almost at arm's length from the detectives as they watched from a window.

'What do we do now?' yelled Vasily, as they waited for the jets to die down.

'Retire to a safe distance and watch ... that's what we seem to do most of the time,' Alexei added rather despondently.

They waited until the steps were run up to the Tupolev's door and watched as the trickle of passengers swelled to a flood across the tarmac apron.

35

'Here they come – tweed suits and woollen jackets!' chuckled Vasily.

'And no sunglasses or raffia handbags,' added Pudovkin.

Dealing as they did with the central area of Moscow, with its tourist hotels, they prided themselves that they could tell the nationality of any visitor by appearances. Though they exaggerated a great deal, the twinsets and cardigans of the British women and the solid, subdued suiting of the men could usually be distinguished from the more flamboyant trappings of the Americans.

One section of the plane's load were obviously British.

'That must be their "keeper" – that tall one,' observed Vasily, nodding in the direction of Gilbert Bynge, who was rounding up his charges like a sheepdog at a country show.

'I wonder which is *our* man?' mused Pudovkin, 'Let's get into a corner and look inconspicuous.'

They retired to a couple of easy chairs in a corner, where the broad red stripe down their trousers could not be seen, and picked up copies of *Izvestia* and *Komsomolskaya Pravda* to screen their faces.

The Trans-Europa party joined the shuffle into the reception lounge, fighting their way through the revolving doors.

'Here they come,' muttered Alexei, 'The capitalists coming to brave the terrible Bolsheviks!' His mild sarcasm was without rancour – he appreciated and deplored the gulf that existed between their two worlds.

'That must be Smith,' he suddenly whispered to Vasily, behind their paper screens. 'Ilyichev said he was the only young man apart from the courier – fair wavy hair and good looks. And a scarf around his throat.'

The lieutenant at once spotted the man his chief had singled out, but his gaze was distracted by the glamorous Mrs Treasure, about whom the man Smith was fussing like a bumble-bee. He was trying to carry her case as well as his own two, but she seemed reluctant to part with it.

Pudovkin's practised eye ran over the whole party, but saw little else of interest. They were all middle-aged or elderly, apart from Smith, the girl and the courier. The only other person under forty-five was a tall, bearded man dressed in sloppy, beatnik-style clothes.

Smith looked innocuous enough. He appeared to be in no immediate danger of committing mayhem or arson. Alexei nudged his assistant and they slipped quietly out of the lounge, whilst the tourists still milled around the reception desk.

They went back to their Volga and sat watching while the party came out of the terminal to board their blue Intourist coach.

The procession, headed by three old ladies recently disinterred from a Cheltenham tea shop, came slowly down the steps to the waiting bus, harried by the elegant Gilbert Bynge, complete with fistfuls of new forms and vouchers.

'This must be one of the expensive tours,' commented Vasily. 'The kids and the workers come in larger and cheaper parties – there are only about twenty of these.'

They watched Bynge helping the old ladies up the steps of the coach.

'What now, do we follow that hearse all the way back in second gear?' Moiseyenko sounded aggrieved.

Alexei, who had shrunk back into his overheated overcoat, emerged momentarily. 'No, you can drive at your favourite reckless speed straight back to the Hotel Metropol … I want to get there well ahead of them; we've got some arrangements to make with the manager!'

Chapter Four

Room 513 seemed an oasis of peace after the drive from the airport.

Simon Smith sank into an easy chair with a sigh of relief. His neck was killing him, his feet were aching and his head was reeling with a mixture of genuine headache and the pressure of so many fears.

Liz Treasure was playing up again, after a temporary lapse into tenderness over his misadventure in Finland. She was starting the hard-to-get act again.

After a few moments blissful inertia, Simon painfully raised his head to look at his new quarters. The large room was high and airy, with one long window filling most of the outer wall. Rather Victorian in appearance, in spite of the modern writing desk and twisty wire table lamps, it had a bathroom in one corner, the door being in the L-shaped recess next to the corridor.

The bed was large and soft; it had the usual continental super-eiderdown instead of sheets and blankets.

He looked around uncomprehendingly – these solid signs of normality seemed to make the reality of his terrible position a dream. Yet here he was, a couple of thousand miles from home and God knows how many inside the Iron Curtain, with both a homicidal rival and possibly the Soviet secret police after his blood.

He sighed but it ended in a shudder. Less than twenty-four hours ago he had been sitting in fair contentment in that cafe in Helsinki – then reading that damned newspaper report about Kramer's death seemed to have triggered off disaster.

He touched his neck gingerly, to see how sore it really was. His voice was still hoarse, but the earlier tenderness over his Adam's apple was much less. There were vague bruises there, hidden under a silk cravat, and the muscles creaked when he turned his head.

'Always thought there was loss of memory before unconsciousness,' he muttered bitterly, 'but *I* bloody well didn't get it – I can still feel those fingers going around my throat.'

He shuddered again. Thankfully he had been spared the memory of being tossed into the water and of being fished out of Helsinki harbour like a drowned rat ... the first thing that had come back to him was staring up at a policeman from the floor of a Finnish police wagon on its way to hospital. From then on, his recovery had been rapid and, in spite of efforts by the police and casualty doctor to get him to hospital, he had resolutely insisted on being taken back to the *Yuri Dolgorukiy*. After a night in the sick bay, he had been well enough to walk ashore at Leningrad the next morning.

All he felt now as he slumped in the chair was fatigue, not illness. Even the marathon walk around the corridors of the Hotel Metropol seemed calculated to increase his tiredness. He had stupidly insisted on carrying one of Elizabeth's cases as well as his own, before finding that they had to trudge about half a mile around the fourth floor to get to their rooms. With unfathomable Russian logic, the management had blocked off the main corridor on one side of the lift, so that to reach the rooms immediately behind this partition, one had to walk around four sides of the enormous building to arrive within a dozen yards of the starting point.

All these fatuous thoughts marched through his mind as if to keep out the main nagging fear – who had tried to kill him yesterday?

If there was any silver lining to the black clouds now rolling in on him, it was that the Soviets were unlikely to be responsible – they had no need of back-alley assassination when they were going to get him deep inside their territory within a few hours.

His frantic rationalising was interrupted by a rap on the door. Gilbert Bynge, finding it unlocked, poked his head inside, then bounced in after a quick glance as if to make sure that Simon didn't have Elizabeth Treasure pinned to the bed.

He trotted across the room, waving sheaves of paper.

'Here we are, meal tickets, programmes, maps, leaflets; all sorts of bumf with the compliments of Intourist – and some forms to sign.'

He doled out the documents and then looked casually around the room, his receding chin and prominent nose making him look like a stage characterisation of the idiot English aristocrat.

'Everything OK? ... damn nasty show about the fall you had ... sure you don't want me to get a quack to see you again – it's all free; on the house in Russia!'

Simon shook his head, slowly and painfully.

'No, I'm fine, really.'

Gilbert seemed reluctant to leave.

'Funny that you should hit your throat on the jolly old railings and then fall into the drink ... you can't have been sloshed at four in the afternoon, eh?'

He spoke jocularly, but it was apparent that he thought Simon's explanation to be highly unlikely.

Simon grunted. 'I'm that sort of chap – if there's anything to fall over, I'll find it.'

Gilbert grinned feebly. Simon noticed for the first time that he had a small tic, a slight twitch of the corner of the mouth every moment or two.

'The room seems all right' he said, as the courier made no move to go.

'As long as you don't drown again in the damn great bath,' Gilbert haw-hawed. 'You want to watch the flush, too, some of 'em go off like depth charges!'

He turned to the door at last, then looked back.

'Hope you appreciate the way I fixed the room numbers.' He cast a roguish eye at the communicating door leading to Liz Treasure's room, and gave a leer.

Simon grunted again – he was in no mood for salacious chit-chat. 'Thanks – I'll stand you a drink on it sometime – is all the party up on this floor?'

Gilbert smirked and his mouth twitched again, 'Only the elite – the "hoi polloi" are downstairs.'

'Who do you reckon are the elite?'

'Yourself, of course … Mrs Treasure, the "reverend gentleman", our little Swiss chappie, "Arty" Shaw – when he's sober – and a couple of the less senile old dears – and yours truly,' he added without modesty.

He moved a little nearer the door. 'I'll hold you to the offer of that drink later on – there's no bar, by the way. In Russia, you have to sit down in the restaurant to tipple – the stuff they sell makes it advisable, anyway!'

He actually opened the door and said his last piece – 'Cheerio, hope the old neck improves.'

Waving his papers with a flourish that almost screamed 'anyone for tennis?' he vanished, leaving Simon's jangling nerves that much more tense.

'Blasted idiot!' he mumbled after him, 'Pseudo-Oxford accent and the brains of a peacock.'

He settled back to continue his gloomy stocktaking of the crisis.

He was being got at, in a big way, but by whom? Must be someone in the Trans-Europa party … the same one that knocked off Harry Lee Kramer and searched his own flat the following night. Again, equally clearly, the same person turned over his cabin on the ship two nights before.

But who – who – who?

He called down into the deep recesses of his jittery brain, but answer came there none.

Not finding a 'who', Simon turned to the 'why' and the 'how' of it all. The first question seemed straightforward enough – if it wasn't the Committee of State Security, it must be a competitor for the tool steel. Kramer had hinted as much in the Happy Dragon … who had he mentioned; the Germans and someone else? The French, of course.

French – Fragonard! The two names slipped together like fish and chips or Laurel and Hardy – yet it seemed ridiculous to accuse the portly little Swiss of murder just because he was the only one with a Gallic name. *And anyway, the poor little guy is too short to reach up to my neck*!

Yet the nagging suspicion would not leave him and, with no German in the Party, Fragonard remained as a possible.

Simon swore as logic fought with prejudice 'I'm working for the Yanks, but God knows I'm no American, so why should he work for the French – and, hell, he's Swiss!'

He left the problem, to think about the 'how'.

At first sight it seemed impossible that the killer of Kramer could murder one night and be on the ship after Simon the very next day, unless he had booked up in advance.

He suddenly realized that Fragonard had not joined the *Yuri* the next day, in fact. He had come aboard at Copenhagen, two days later! His intuition about the voluble Swiss flooded back in force.

But why had Kramer been done away with? Simon mulled this one over again, getting almost masochistic delight in frightening himself mortal.

'They knew what Kramer wanted and who he was sending to get it – but perhaps they didn't know the local

43

arrangements in Moscow ... all this guff about the German chap, Pabst, and the place I'm supposed to make contact. What if they wrung the truth out of Kramer and killed him in the process – or disposed of him afterwards to keep his mouth shut?'

It seemed an extreme way to go about getting a few grammes of steel, but there it was ... worth millions to an industrial consortium, who would not want to know the details of how it was obtained, as long as they got the precious end product.

The same old thoughts tramped in a heavy-footed circle through Simon's mind as he sat morosely in his chair. He always came back to the same starting point – who was trying to eliminate him and what could he do about it?

Too late, he bemoaned his stupidity and stubbornness in not cutting his losses in Helsinki and flying home from there ... especially as he'd had another chance after the attack, when he could have stayed in hospital and salved his pride as the ship sailed without him – his shocked state must have turned his brain, he thought, looking back.

Now he was stuck for ten days in a hostile country, virtually imprisoned with someone bent on murdering him.

There was no way out; he could hardly go and pour out his heart to Gilbert and ask for an air flight straight home from Moscow. Gilbert Bynge? ... in his present suspicious mood, he began to wonder about Gilbert. A courier for years on the Russian route, every opportunity to go to and fro across the frontiers. He spoke perfect Russian, had been at the game for years ... what *about* Gilbert? Far from trusting him to get Simon out of this jam, should he put him well up the list of suspects?

Bynge certainly had the physique to have done that nasty bit of work on the Helsinki quayside – thin but tall, and with youth on his side. Apart from Fragonard, there were no other likely candidates, apart from the dipsomaniac Irishman, Michael Shaw, the vicar and the old ladies. And of course, Liz ... she was a big girl, but ...

Simon shrugged off the thought as soon as it entered his mind – apart from his emotions, hadn't she been the one who had helped drag him out of the water?

'Ah, to blazes with it!' he snarled suddenly and jumped up, wincing at the pain in his neck. He went to the window and threw open the double-layered casement, a protection against the Moscow winters. He had to lean well out over the wide sill to see anything.

Immediately below him was the cliff-like wall of the hotel, falling four storeys to the ground below. His room was at the back of the Metropol almost at the northern corner. To his left was a busy shopping street leading away from Sverdlov Square. The rumble of traffic, the crowded pavements, the ice cream stalls and the shops could have been almost any city in Europe.

Below and to his right was a high curved wall of ancient red brick, with a curious Oriental battlement along the top. From previous readings of his guidebook, he recognized this as part of the Chinese Wall, a remnant of the old city fortifications. It ran now from some stable-like buildings a few yards away to meet the hotel wall just below Liz Treasure's room, separating the street from the rough ground that formed the Metropol's backyard.

His inspection of the outer world complete, he pulled his head in and closed the windows. The next half-hour passed in unpacking his two cases into the cavernous wardrobe and in risking life and limb with bath taps and flush. They at least took his mind off things for a time, but afterwards the worries came back in full spate.

Ought he to sit tight and do nothing, or should he try to finish off the job on the principle of being hung for a sheep instead of a lamb?

His mental ferment was interrupted by a tap at the door. He had locked it against the murderous Mr. 'X' when

45

Gilbert left and now he hurried to the half-inch gap down the side of the worn woodwork.

'Who's there?'

'Me ... Liz, you idiot. What's the idea of barricading yourself in?' The handle rattled impatiently as he dropped his hand to the key.

Elizabeth Treasure had also bathed and changed and now stood there looking ravishing in a simple, but slinky white dress.

'You're taking me down to lunch,' she said. It was a statement, not an invitation or request. 'They eat here until teatime, I'm told, so we're not too late.'

Simon looked at his watch and saw with astonishment that it was almost two thirty. Liz had walked past him into the room. He pushed the door shut and followed her, slipping his arms around her waist and kissing the back of her neck. She neither repulsed him nor responded, but stood staring at the communicating door.

'That's Gilbert's little joke,' said Simon.

'If you've any ideas, then forget them,' she said crisply, 'There's a damned great wardrobe against my side!'

Then, to Simon's relief, she actually giggled. Recovering her poise immediately, she dropped her handbag and gloves onto the bed, Turning, she slipped her arms around his neck and kissed him with open-lipped enthusiasm for a full half-minute.

Surprised, but gratified beyond measure, Simon responded avidly. When his hands had slipped down her shoulders to what she evidently considered the Plimsoll line of propriety, she pulled away and went to the mirror. Her very pale lipstick had survived any major damage, so she calmly walked to the bed and picked up her belongings.

'Ready?' she said.

Two hours later, Simon was back in his room, lying on the bed in his underpants. His neck was still sore, but he felt better all round.

The lunch had been lengthy, due to the traditional lethargy of the waiters, but he had enjoyed every minute. Liz had played footsie and rubbed her knee against his for most of the time. Although she was outwardly as impassive as ever, he at last felt that things were moving in the right direction. The fatal lure of sex, which can turn a man's mind away from even the basic rules of survival, had made him forget any ideas of scampering back to London.

After lunch, which had lasted until nearly four o'clock, Gilbert had shepherded the rest of the tour off on a walk around the Kremlin and Red Square, only a few yards from the Metropol. Only Simon and the red-faced Irishman had opted out, the latter without any attempt at excuse, though Simon untruthfully pleaded the after-effects of his 'accident'. In reality, he wanted more time in which to think and perhaps act.

Before lying down to do the thinking part, he had prowled around the room, rather shamefacedly looking for hidden microphones. He looked everywhere and found only a complete absence of dust. The only mysterious object was a current fixture list for Sheffield Wednesday Football Club, hidden at the back of a drawer!

Flat on the bed, he thought over the past day and some confidence crept back into his soul, born mainly of the complete normality of things since leaving the ship.

His self-congratulation over, he came down to the task of deciding about Gustav Pabst, the renegade engineer at the automobile works. Should he try to contact him, or was it too risky in the circumstances? Simon was still convinced, almost intuitively, that the Soviet authorities were so far uninvolved in the conspiracy. Naively, he thought that they had had no reason yet to take any notice

47

of him. So as long as he could keep clear of Mr 'X', he should be reasonably safe. There was another two thousand pounds at stake – the fact that Kramer was dead was irrelevant, as the American had arranged for Simon to contact someone else on his return to London. Presumably Harry Lee had only been one cog in a large and efficient American machine, so if Simon could deliver the goods, the cash would be there just the same.

With his hands behind his head, he stared at the high ceiling and made his decision. For some reason – perhaps not unconnected with Liz Treasure – he had calmed down a lot since the morning and was more prepared to take a chance.

I was shot at a damn sight more in Cyprus, for less money in a year than I'll get for a couple of hours effort here, he reasoned, trying to convince himself that he was doing the right thing.

He swung himself up to sit on the edge of the bed, and decided to have a shot at it.

Now that he had made up his mind, he settled down to devise a plan of action for 'Operation Tool Steel.'

Chapter Five

The same afternoon, whilst the British party were marching around the Kremlin behind an attractive Intourist guide, Alexei Pudovkin was in his office in Petrovka.

He sat in his partitioned box, jacket on the back of his chair, earnestly studying a long telegram from Leningrad. Periodically, he looked up to curse the central heating, which for some reason could not be turned off, though the sun was streaming through the dusty windows.

If Ilyichev had been cryptically brief in his first cable, he had made up for it in the second, which was almost a letter.

Alexei skimmed through it once, then settled down for a more thorough study. He had a bottle of mineral water to sustain him and he sipped this slowly as he digested the new information from the Hero City. Halfway through, there was a perfunctory rap on his door and Vasily Moiseyenko breezed in, laden with papers.

'The stuff from visa office, *tovarishch* ... nothing of any help, as far as I can see.'

'Sit down – have some water.'

Pudovkin didn't look up, but pushed the bottle across. The young lieutenant perched himself on the corner of the desk – the only other chair was piled high with papers from other cases, swept off Pudovkin's desk to make way for the 'Great New Case'. He waited in silence for about a minute, then his patience expired.

'That from Ilyichev?' Alexei grunted.

'Anything good in it?'

'Tell you in a minute – just shut up, will you?'

Vasily grinned … the scrawny old bear was always like this when he was happy with some work. If he was polite and talkative, it usually meant that he was bored.

Eventually, the older man threw the message form down and creaked his back up to a more erect position.

'Want to know what's in it, eh, Vasily Sergeivich?'

'Bursting! … what's it all about?'

Pudovkin took another swig of water with exasperating slowness.

'This man Smith … Simon Smith …' he began.

'Looked like a proper ladies' man to me.'

Alexei glared at his assistant. 'Who's telling this, eh? … this man Smith goes ashore yesterday when the ship calls at Helsinki and is brought back in an ambulance at the last moment.'

He looked at the cable again 'One of the women in the party – a woman called Treasure – found him floating unconscious in the harbour. He later told the ship's doctor that he slipped on the wet cobbles, hit his neck on the railings and can't remember any more. The Finnish authorities only know that he was fished out of the water half-drowned.'

He stopped for some mineral water.

'The important thing is the ship's surgeon said that he had marks on his neck typical of those of strangulation!'

Moiseyenko tut-tutted, his face gleaming with anticipation. 'Attempted murder!' he said gleefully.

Pudovkin shrugged, a gesture which made him look like a lean old vulture.

'Perhaps so – but there's more. The doctor and the chief officer searched his cabin, after reporting to the captain of the ship – Smith was away in the sick berth – they found an automatic pistol hidden under his mattress.'

Vasily's bland round face opened up in surprise. 'What's the game – trying to start a counter-revolution?'

Alexei smiled crookedly. 'The ship reported it to Leningrad Marine Radio, they put him through to the militia ... whether the KGB got in on the act as well, I don't know – I certainly don't propose to tell them.'

He sniffed and carried on. 'After a night in the sickbay, Smith rapidly improved and insisted on going back to his cabin to pack. After he left the ship this morning, they searched again and found the gun still in the same place.'

Vasily frowned. 'So has he committed any offence – yet?'

'As far as I see – no. He didn't bring the gun into the country and although the ship is legally Russian soil, passengers are not challenged about contraband until they actually land.'

'Why bring it so far and then leave it?'

'You're full of blasted questions today ... d'you think I'm a fortune-teller or something? ... all I can think is that he got scared of having attention drawn to him over the Helsinki brawl and decided not to risk smuggling the pistol.'

'So what is he – a spy?'

Pudovkin rocked back on his chair as far as the cramped space would allow.

'Again, I don't know. He may even be one of ours, I suppose – the Cheka never let their right hand know what the left is doing.'

Moiseyenko was serious and silent at the mention of the 'others'.

'If you think that, Alexei Alexandrovich, why not turn it over to the grey men from Dzerzhinsky Square?'[4]

Pudovkin shook his head doggedly. '*You're* changing your tune, lad – I thought you wanted to hang on to the job ... and until Fat Father upstairs says otherwise, we carry on.'

---

[4]Headquarters of the KGB.-

He had a last swig of mineral water. 'And I've got a feeling about this one, Vasily – let's just play it by ear, eh?'

Simon sat in his room, biting his fingernails in indecision. Every fibre in his aching body cried out to either finish the job or get the hell out of the Soviet Union.

He went to the window and stared out over the canyon which separated his room from the big children's store across the street. He smoothed a hand wearily over his springy well-groomed hair and wondered how to go about contacting Pabst. Telephone and telegram were too risky, so the only thing left was to go and see the man.

With almost a convulsion of decision, he swung around to the wardrobe and took out his light raincoat. Hurrying now, as if not to give himself time to change his mind, he fled to the door and strode away down the corridor.

In the lift, he said nothing to the impassive old woman who operated it, but merely jerked a thumb downwards.

As the slow box lumbered down, the fear of being watched flooded back into his mind. Although he was still blissfully unaware of the Militia's interest in him, he was still worried about his murderous competitor. The last thing he wanted was to lead 'Mr X' straight to Gustav Pabst, to say nothing of the risk of being waylaid again in some back street. By the time the gates opened on the ground floor, he had a plan of sorts ready in his mind.

Instead of making for the steps down into the hotel foyer, he left the lift and casually turned left into the short passage that led to the restaurant. He walked into the huge dining room and kept on along the side wall in the direction of the glass doors that led to the kitchens. As he reached them, he was gratified to see a worn wooden swing-door just inside the glass, on the opposite wall to the serving area. There were a few late patrons about, but no staff. Without the hesitation that gives away a timid trespasser, Simon boldly pushed open the glass doors, turned right and marched straight through the wooden one.

His gamble had paid off. He found himself in a gloomy corridor piled with crates and boxes of vegetables. It was the store department and should have a rear goods entrance somewhere.

In the distance, he saw figures moving about. As an impromptu camouflage, he picked up the nearest box and with this clasped to his chest, strode briskly down the long passage towards a gleam of daylight from an open door. He nodded as he passed the storemen, but they hardly spared him a glance. In a few seconds, he was out of the building, blinking in the daylight of the backyard. The cobbled area had a high wall in which were set big gates, now standing wide open. He dumped his box on the back of a parked lorry and walked out into a lane, where he found himself looking at the traffic of 25th of October Street.

Remembering his much-studied street map, he turned right and soon was at Sverdlov Square Metro station.

He bought a five kopek ticket at the automatic machines and read that it would take him anywhere on the Metro system.

In the ornate marble palace below, he boarded the first train that came, changed at the next station and repeated this at the next. On both occasions, he was certain that no one had followed him, so he studied his pocket chart of the Metro system and caught a train for the terminus of the south-eastern line, the Avtozavodskayastation. It was a long ride and he sat in the spotless carriage, half-empty just before the rush hour, and marvelled at the superb construction of the Moscow Underground. Free from the grime, the advertisements and the squalor of the London system, it had an almost cathedral-like atmosphere – the crystal chandeliers of some stations, the rows of statues in others seemed more like a religious or cultural monument than a transport utility.

It was getting on for four thirty when he came up to street level again. He made his way as quickly as his poor knowledge of the suburbs allowed. Most of the people about seemed to be old women and children going home from school. He asked several old ladies and eventually found his way to Borovitskaya Avenue. It looked exactly the same as a hundred other streets in the locality, great rectangular blocks of yellow-grey apartment buildings lining wide tree-lined boulevards. Trams ran up the side of the roads and at intervals the flats were interrupted by shopping areas and cinemas.

Finding the right block and then the section of the block was almost as hard as discovering the street, but eventually he arrived at a ground-floor doorway with 'Fourth Entrance' written over it. Still memorising the address given to him in the Happy Dragon, he climbed the stairs to the third floor. The bleak concrete and plaster contrasted strongly with the deep carpeting of his own London flat and he went faster as if to speed his return to those more luxurious surroundings.

On the sixth landing, there was a glass door with one pane broken. He saw a bell push at the edge, but tried the door first. It opened and he went in to the smell of cooking.

The sound of a child wailing led him to a row of doors along one side of a passage. Through one of them, he saw two women working at a row of gas stoves in a large communal kitchen. He was just going to rap on the door panel when a voice behind scared him almost to death.

'What do you want, *grazhdanin*?'[5]

---

[5]Citizen

54

A young woman stood watching him. She held a small girl in her arms, the child's head wrapped in a towel, with strands of wet dark hair stuck around her wide eyes.

Simon recovered his poise and replied in his best Russian. He hoped the woman would take his accent to be German, like Pabst's.

'Ah, I was trying to find the apartment of my friend Gustav Pabst – I think he lives in Number 12.'

The woman's suspicious face relaxed – *perhaps she thought me a prowler or thief*, thought Simon.

'He's still at work … at the Likachev factory,' she said.

Simon's heart sank – it was gone five o'clock now; he'd hoped that Pabst might have finished on a four p.m. shift. 'What time will he be home, citizeness?'

'Usually about eighteen thirty – his wife comes at the same time, she works in the canteen there.'

The young woman was very pretty, Simon realized suddenly. The libertine in him was unquenchable, even in times of stress like this. He shrugged the thought away. 'I can't wait … perhaps I could leave a note under his door.'

The child began to wail and her mother bumped her down on to her feet.

'Go and see grandmother – go on!'

She stood up, her figure straining against her blouse. Simon tore his gaze away.

'It's his day off tomorrow – he'll be home then,' she volunteered.

Simon shook his head 'Thanks, I'll have to leave a note – it's too far to come again.'

The woman pointed out the door to Number 12, further down the corridor, then ran into the kitchen to scold her daughter.

Simon walked to Pabst's door and saw a noticeboard just outside. It held a ragged cluster of pamphlets and notices exhorting the inhabitants to this and that extra effort for the State. He pulled down one which invited them to become voluntary bricklayers at a new sports stadium and used the back of it to write a short anonymous note to Pabst. He asked him to come to a certain rendezvous the next morning or, if that was impossible, at the same time the following day, bringing his 'goods' with him.

Simon printed it in German, doing his best to disguise the lettering as much as possible. Slipping it under the door, he made his way out, smiling at the young woman with undisguised approval as he passed the kitchen door.

The homecoming workers were crowding the streets and the Metro on the return journey. Relief at not being followed was tempered by the limited success of his mission. If the East German failed to keep his date the following day, Simon would have to decide whether to risk another delay until the alternative rendezvous on Wednesday … if he didn't show up then, that was it as far as Simon was concerned; he had stuck his neck out far enough. As he went up the steps of the Metropol, he decided that if Pabst didn't come up to scratch, his neck would suffer an acute relapse. With luck, he could be airborne on his way to Heathrow by Wednesday evening, and the tool steel could go to the devil.

Chapter Six

Dinner that evening was an enjoyable meal, as far as Simon Smith was concerned. His efforts to contact Pabst had at least given him the feeling that he was doing something, and he felt the better for it.

The fifth floor members of the Trans-Europa party gravitated to the same table. The two old ladies went across to join some even more senile friends, so the group came to consist of Elizabeth, Simon, Gilbert, the benign, if inarticulate, priest, an already intoxicated Michael Shaw, the portly Fragonard and one of the Intourist guides, a pretty dark girl whom Gilbert had produced from the hotel bureau, with his international flair for obtaining attractive companions.

The dining room, looking to Simon like a Victorian airship hangar lined with potted plants and be-flagged tables, was crowded. It was filled with the buzz of conversation and the excellent music from a six-piece orchestra. As the meal was again a prolonged affair, there was plenty of time for dancing between the courses. The cultural thaw was not so pronounced in the centre of Moscow as on the *Yuri Dolgorukiy* and the beat and twist numbers were watered down to sedate foxtrots and waltzes, but Gilbert, the Intourist girl and Liz and Simon enjoyed themselves well enough. Even the rotund and un-sinister-looking Jules Fragonard took the floor with Elizabeth – the only static ones were the rather overawed reverend and Michael Shaw, who could probably not even stand, let alone dance.

He sat with a benign, glazed smile on his face, steadily working his way through a bottle of Hungarian *Barack Pálinka*. He would answer direct questions in monosyllables, but otherwise was a social blank.

While Liz was away dancing with the little Swiss chap, Simon studied the red-headed Irishman with curious interest. No one knew much about him except that he was 'arty' … what this meant, Simon wasn't sure. He knew that someone had mentioned that he was a writer, but whether of newspaper advertisements or poetry, he knew not. 'Another Dublin Yeats, perhaps,' he murmured to himself, then aloud, to the bearded man, 'This a pure holiday or are you getting atmosphere for a novel?'

Two red-rimmed eyes swivelled across at him and a crack appeared in the tangled red beard to show a loose-lipped grin. 'No bloody holiday, son!' came the enigmatic answer, borne on a blast of liquor fumes.

'Heard you were a writer,' persisted Simon; the vicar looked at them benevolently, almost pathetically eager to be 'one of the boys'.

Michael Shaw made a revolting, derisive noise in his throat. 'Writer, my ass! … I make a few bob by prostituting the English language once a week for the Fleet Street slave masters – my *real* job is drinking.'

This was a long speech for him and he subsided into his glass almost immediately. Simon gave up, and turned to watch the seductive figure of Liz Treasure swaying back through the crowd towards him. She was another enigma in her own way – he had tried hard to fathom out the 'Mrs' angle, but still she evaded telling him whether she was widowed, divorced, or just married. He knew she kept a smart boutique in Chelsea, in partnership with a friend, but that was about as far as his knowledge went … apart from her admitting to being twenty-five. Another odd thing about her was that blasted suitcase. On three separate occasions, he had helped her with her luggage and each time she had become quite annoyed when he had tried to carry her older brown valise – in the airport at Leningrad, when he had accidently tripped over it, she had become almost incoherent with temper. *A funny girl*, he thought – *but, oh, what a shape*! He hissed through his teeth as he watched her, as if letting off the excess pressure that the sight of her engendered in him.

By ten thirty, the party began to break up. They had all eaten and drunk too much, even the vicar, who left first. He was followed shortly after by Monsieur Fragonard, who made effusive apologies and kissed Liz's hand with too much relish for Simon's liking.

Shaw fell asleep across the table and was still there when Simon managed to prise Liz away at about eleven o'clock. Gilbert and the Russian girl were dancing the last waltz as they left.

The 'widow', as he had hopefully come to think of Liz, was reluctant to leave but was in a slightly giggly state, and could not hold out against Simon's persuasion for long.

He had felt distinctly fuzzy himself for some time, but had got a second wind after missing a couple of rounds of vodka and, with an air of grim purpose, piloted her to the lift.

The old lady in black – presumably a different one from the morning, but they all looked alike – took them up with an impassive, averted face, as he held Liz tightly around the shoulders whilst she put her arms around his waist. Such open amorousness was distinctly uncultured in the Soviet Union and they got another severe look from the grim old woman who handed them their keys at the floor desk when they left the lift.

They began the marathon walk around the corridors. Around the first bend, Liz leant heavily against him, singing a little song. At the next corner, he put his arm around her and when they entered the home straight, she pulled off her high-heeled sandals and swung them gaily as they weaved their way irregularly towards Rooms 513 and 514.

Without any pretence at subtlety, Simon stuck his key in his own door and almost bundled her inside, kicking it shut behind him. She said nothing as he aimed her at the bed, and in fact waltzed toward it, flopping down on her back and throwing her shoes up in the air with a tipsy laugh.

I hope to hell she isn't going to pass out on me, he prayed, as he slid down alongside her and began to kiss her lips with a fervour that was part passion and part relief that no one had tried to murder him that evening.

A creature of extreme moods, she responded avidly. They devoured each other for a few moments, then she pulled his head down on to the wide expanse of smooth skin exposed by her fairly low-cut dress. She kissed and nibbled his ear, giggling occasionally, and sometimes whispering something to him.

He took no notice at first – some of it was semi-erotic endearments, but there was something else – mixed up with giggles and over-dramatic emphasis. 'Mmmmm – darling Simon, I've been beastly to you, poor dear. Nearly got drowned and I was so *nasty* to you.'

She nuzzled him again, and he was so overcome with sensual abandon that the words just buzzed through his head without his mind taking a grip on them. 'Mmm, you're going to help me, aren't you, darling Simon … I'm not just a silly old tourist, I'm here on deadly secret business …'

She bit his ear violently and went off into peals of laughter.

He dropped abruptly from the clouds to wonder what the silly beautiful bitch was talking about, then a fresh attack of writhing and wide-lipped kissing drove all other thoughts but sex from his mind.

And then came the knock on the door.

At about the time the dinner party was breaking up in the Metropol, Alexei Pudovkin again sat hunched over his desk in Petrovka. He had a telephone to his ear. Vasily Moiseyenko, a cardboard-stemmed cigarette hanging from his lips, sat as usual on the desk, his legs swinging as he watched the old man's lined face.

After a moment, the captain dropped the receiver into its cradle with a final grunt, and stretched his long legs under the table.

'Time to go home, lad.'

'That was the Metropol, I take it?'

'Yes, Yelena Voronina – a good girl, that. She hasn't had a very exciting time today, but monitoring the hotel phones is a change from spotting pickpockets in the GUM stores.'

Vasily's attractive face split into a grin. 'She's a girl all right ... if I wasn't a confirmed bachelor and she wasn't married, I might get ideas about Woman Officer Voronina!'

Alexei grunted again, his mind suddenly full of Darya's scolding.

'Leave them all alone, son – you can get all you want without actually marrying them.'

His voice was bitter and the young lieutenant was wise enough to say nothing for the moment.

'So what's the score?' he asked after a long silence, 'Do we just go home – what did she have to say?'

Alexei rocked his chair back against his filing cabinets. 'They're all there, having a good time. Some are just off to bed. Nothing to report, except one curious thing ... our man, this Simon Smith, was seen coming back into the Metropol at about six o'clock, though no one had seen him go out! Nothing else suspicious, but we haven't any idea where he went.'

Moiseyenko raised his eyebrows. 'But we had a chap sitting in the foyer from the time they arrived from the airport – didn't he spot him going out?'

'No – Yelena says that he swears blind that Smith didn't pass him – and he had him pointed out at lunch, so he could recognise him.'

'Who was it?'

'Lev Pomansky – your old pal.'

Moiseyenko snorted derisively. 'That old clodhopper! He wouldn't notice a suspect if they were to tread on his feet as they left!'

Alexei smiled tolerantly. The ambitious, impatient Moiseyenko always took the chance to needle old Pomansky, who made up for his admitted lack of brilliance by good humour and dogged devotion.

'So now we just go home, none the wiser as to what it's all about?'

Pudovkin nodded his grey cropped head. 'Carry on all night with the surveillance and the telephone watch – Yelena finishes at midnight ... I've left another man to relieve Pomansky at ten. If there are any calls from Smith's room extension, the night switchboard operator has orders to call our man in to listen to them at once.'

'I hope he understands English,' said Vasily quickly.

Pudovkin glowered at him. 'Look, sonny, I was at this game for years before your curly little head ever appeared in the nursery, so don't try to teach me now, eh?'

Vasily grinned back impudently. 'I'll catch you out one day, Alexei Alexandrovich!'

Pudovkin stared at his protégé, sensing his impatience with old frumps like himself and Pomansky, who had never got above lieutenant in twenty-four years' service.

He got up suddenly ... he wasn't going to get senile, by damn he wasn't! Not to please Moiseyenko or anyone else. He still had eight years before he need retire and he was going to make the most of them – starting now!

'Let's have a last walk around there before we go home – we can get the Metro from Sverdlov Square.'

They walked in silence down Petrovka Street, now quiet except for the occasional car or taxi. The homeward surge from cinema and theatre was over; they started and finished earlier than their Western counterparts. As they passed the great bulk of the Bolshoi Theatre, the imposing portico was shuttered and silent beneath the prancing horse statues that stood above them, clearly bathed in the yellow light that still came from the western horizon.

Sverdlov Square was still busy and they waited for the traffic lights before crossing the wide street to the Metropol.

'Can't imagine living anywhere but Moscow, can you?' said Moiseyenko, intuitively tuning himself to the old man's thoughts and nostalgic mood.

Pudovkin sighed, but it was contentment, for once. Here he was *really* home, amongst the streets and pavements of Moscow – far more so than up in his office or home at the apartment, where Darya dominated every tense moment.

'I did seven years on the beat in Central Division,' he said, as they crossed on the green light. 'Every corner, every alley almost, has a story I could tell – nowhere like old Moskva!'

Like half a million other city policemen the world over, each thought that their own 'manor' was unique – their proprietary patch, loved and sometimes hated for the evils it contained or the drudgery it provided.

They strolled under the dark window-studded precipice that was the front of the hotel and reached the rather insignificant main entrance. A relic from long before the Revolution, the Metropol was far inferior to the 'wedding cake' showpieces put up by Stalin, like the Peking or the Ukraina, but inside it still had a charm of its own.

They came through the tall glass doors into the foyer. The newspaper and picture postcard stalls were closed and the Intourist bureau was in darkness, but a few people still sat around under the old chandeliers. As they entered, a group of men came down the steps from the restaurant carrying violin cases: the orchestra finished well before midnight, Pudovkin remembered.

He looked around and saw a burly figure seated in a corner. He wore a plastic mackintosh and was unsuccessfully trying to hide the broad red stripe of his militia trousers beneath a coffee table. Alexei sighed and beckoned him over.

'Why don't you stick your whistle in your mouth and hold up a placard saying "Militia"?' snapped the captain, sarcastically. 'You look about as inconspicuous as a firing squad over there.'

'Probably doing what that fool Pomansky told him,' cut in Moiseyenko nastily.

The militiaman, young and untried, shuffled his feet awkwardly and Pudovkin, recollecting his own shortcomings when a recruit, softened his voice.

'Get over there behind the reception desk – take that coat off and scrounge a porter's jacket. Your pants won't be seen behind the counter.'

The solitary woman behind the desk lifted the flap for them, then went incuriously back to her book – disinterest in law enforcement was built-in to every Russian above middle age.

'Nothing happened since you've been on?' Pudovkin asked the militiaman.

The young patrolman shook his head; he had been taken off his night beat for this and was mystified and uneasy. 'The man that Pomansky pointed out to me went upstairs with an Englishwoman about eleven – they'd been drinking a bit.'

'No sign of him since?'

'Not a thing.'

'Any phone calls?' cut in Vasily, determined to flash his rank.

'No – not all day, so Woman Officer Voronina said – not since the listening watch was set up, anyway.'

Pudovkin nodded. As soon as they had left the airport that morning, they had come to see the manager of the Metropol to arrange for round-the-clock observation of Simon Smith.

A militia engineer had come to fix a special circuit from the big telephone switchboard, which could tap any of the room phones of the Trans-Europa party and make a permanent record on a tape recorder. The apparatus was installed in a corner of the exchange room behind the reception desk. The manager seemed most unhappy at the prospect – his uneasiness, unknown to the detectives, was due to the fact that a similar request, or rather command, had been made some hours earlier and, in fact, another listening team was already installed in the basement. The operators had offered the manager an unpleasant fate if he revealed their presence to anyone, *including* the Moscow Militia.

Elizabeth Treasure couldn't have been as tipsy as Simon had thought. Immediately after the knock came on the door, she sat bolt upright on the bed, said an extremely rude word and hurriedly began to do up the top buttons of her dress.

Simon's feverish mood deflated as rapidly as a punctured tyre. He cursed and pushed himself up on one hand on the side of the bed, glowering at the door as if daring it to make more noise. It dared. A rapid urgent tattoo echoed through the high-ceilinged room.

'Ignore it and they'll go away,' he hissed to Liz, though he knew it was now a waste of time to try to salvage the operation – the interruption had broken the thread of

65

passion and their risen sap was falling fast. Her lipstick and her hair were mussed, even one false eyelash hung awry. The magic of the moment was killed stone-dead.

'You'll have to answer it,' she said petulantly, as a third rapping clattered on the panels.

Spitting tin-tacks, Simon climbed out of bed and ran hasty fingers through his tumbled hair. He feebly tried to straighten the scarf around his neck and smooth down his crumpled suit. Forcing his feet into his shoes, he stumbled to the door.

'What is it – who's there?'

'Please open – it is I, Fragonard.'

With a groan, followed by a sudden mental flash of apprehension, Simon put his hand on the knob, then looked over his shoulder. From the door, the edge of the bathroom cut off all but the foot of the bed. He opened it, to be confronted by the very sober and unusually business-like figure of Monsieur Fragonard. The Swiss seemed to have lost all his benign rotundity, and to the still bemused Simon, he looked somehow menacing in spite of his small size and ridiculous goatee.

'What is it – it's very late?' He felt in his bones that this was no social call.

'I have a matter of the utmost importance to discuss with you, Mr Smith – may I enter?' he said pedantically.

'It's very inconvenient at the moment,' replied Simon. As soon as the words were out of his mouth, he knew he had been tricked. Fragonard had spoken in Russian and he had automatically answered in the same language. There was a gleam of triumph in the other man's eyes and he hazily realized that he had been outmanoeuvred in some way. Fragonard peered beneath the arm that Simon still had on the door. Though he could see nothing, there was a sudden distinct creaking of bed springs and a muttered 'Damn' as Elizabeth dropped her compact. The visitor gave a quick man-of-the-world nod of understanding.

'I apologise for my intrusion – but the matter *is* urgent. Could you come to my room for a few moments?'

There was a sudden cold spot in the middle of Simon's chest. He tried to bluff it out.

'Look here, it's getting on for midnight – can't it wait until morning?'

Fragonard smiled icily. His mouth moved in a brief travesty of humour; he was a different man from an hour ago. 'I think not – it should have been said before.' A pause – they were speaking English again now – then the shot right between Simon's eyes. 'I think Mr Kramer would have understood.'

Simon felt as if a handful of ice cubes had been stuffed down his neck. He stood transfixed, savouring the horrible flavour of the past tense that Fragonard had used over Kramer.

Then he turned, almost shut the door in the other man's face and walked back into the bedroom. As he opened his mouth to speak, Liz beat him to it. 'Don't worry about me, I'm off! One reputation is enough to lose in a night. Caught red-handed – almost,' she added with a touch of regret.

Simon murmured something vague about seeing her later, then walked out to Fragonard.

Without a word, the little man marched in front of his own room, Number 515, two doors further up the corridor.

Inside, it was identical with Simon's, except that it was the other way around – the bathroom was on the left as one went in, instead of on the right.

Fragonard waved him to a chair, but Simon stood obstinately in the middle of the carpet.

'What is all this?' he demanded.

Fragonard took off his jacket and hung it carefully in the wardrobe before answering. He put on a woollen dressing gown of an unlikely tartan pattern over his trousers and shirt, tying up the cord slowly.

67

'I have been all over this room for listening devices – there is nothing, and I am well-versed in these matters.' He waved a hand around the furnishings 'So we may speak freely – only the telephone is dangerous.'

Simon carried on lamely with his innocent act. 'What the devil are you driving at?'

'Let us stop this silly pretence, Mr Smith.' Fragonard sat astride a hard chair near the desk, leaning his arms on the back of it. 'You are young, inexperienced and foolish. Why on earth an old hand like Kramer picked an amateur for an important job like this, I cannot understand – perhaps it *was* time he left the business.'

His voice was insulting in its tone and matched his pale eyes, which sat in his face like polished marbles in a pink blancmange.

Simon said nothing – he felt cold, frightened and utterly disillusioned.

'To save your breath in any further denials, I will tell you that you were to contact Gustav Pabst, who lives in Borovitskaya Avenue 89, and his telephone number is 39-24-59.'

Simon stared at Jules Honore Fragonard and swallowed. He had nothing to say.

The fat man rocked gently to and fro on his chair and gave a smile that almost had some of his old humour in it. He seemed to be enjoying himself.

'To complete the picture, you have been paid a thousand pounds and were to have got another two on delivery of the steel in London.'

'What d'you mean – *were* to have got?' snapped Simon defiantly.

The mention of his money had snapped him out of his paralysis. 'Have you been sent to replace Kramer?'

Fragonard's face darkened as if a shutter had fallen over it.

'You bloody young fool – stupid as well as incompetent.'

Anger began to rise, deep in Simon's soul, but nothing showed yet.

'How do you know all these details then?' he grated.

Fragonard looked at him with contempt 'The same way as you – from Kramer, of course – you idiot! … he told me just before he died.'

Simon digested this and reached a horrifying conclusion. 'You … you killed him!'-His smouldering wrath caught alight, but he kept it screwed down. He had never been closeted with a murderer before.

The Swiss looked modestly at his plump fingers. 'It was unfortunate – after I had got the information from him, Kramer tried to jump me. I had to shoot him. Looking back, it was the best thing. He would only have made trouble, by sending someone after me. That would have been tedious, not like dealing with a bungling amateur like you.'

Simon began to see the inside – his fists opened and closed inside his pockets. Fragonard went on imperturbably.

'You were hardly able to even get this far safely – didn't you fall into the dock in Finland?' His tone was a calculated insult.

Simon took a step nearer and snarled at him.

'Fell? … you damned liar, you know well enough what happened, considering that it was you that half-choked me and then threw me in!'

Fragonard's head jerked up and his eyes needled into Simon's.

'Choked? … what nonsense is this?'

For answer, Simon dragged down one side of his cravat to display the marks on his neck. 'See those … that's what your fat little fingers did. If I'd known it was you, I'd have punched your blasted head all the way from Helsinki to Moscow!'

His temper was welling up now. Far from being a physical coward, his army service had shown that in the heat of the moment, he could be as pugnacious as the next man.

But Fragonard's reaction was curious. He got up from his chair and stood facing Simon. His face seemed a little paler as he said, 'I never left the ship in Finland.' He was not so much defending himself against Simon's accusation as talking to himself. His arrogance had changed to a sudden wariness.

'Are you sure you were attacked?'

'Sure? Of course I'm bloody well sure. Do you think I don't know when I'm attacked from behind, throttled into coma and then half-drowned? I suppose you deny ransacking my flat and my cabin as well!'

Fragonard stared at him. 'In London, yes. I wanted to see if Kramer had given you written instructions about contacting Pabst. It would have saved me killing him for the information ... but on the ship, no – I had no reason to go near your cabin.'

He was rattled now. He stalked up and down on his short legs, smacking a fist into the other palm.

Abruptly he sat down again, with the chair backwards. 'No matter – this is a complication, but is no concern of yours ... in fact *nothing* is a concern of yours! I called you here tonight to make it clear to you.'

'What the hell do you mean?' demanded Simon truculently.

'Keep off! That's what I mean, Mr Smith. I should have warned you to mind your own petty business before you left London, but I got to Kramer too late to book a passage from Tilbury. That's why I had to fly to Copenhagen to join the ship.'

He leant back, holding the chair rail and stared contemptuously at the Englishman 'I repeat, keep off, little boy.'

Simon was speechless with rage for a moment. His slow anger at last was exploded by Fragonard's manner, and eventually he found his tongue 'You cheeky bastard – who d'you think you're ordering about? You've got the bloody nerve to tell me to mind my own business – business that you cut into by way of a murder – to hell with you, chum!'

Fragonard remained impassive, looking up at the enraged man with the same supercilious expression.

'When you have finished your over-dramatised performance, Smith, remember that I shall not hesitate to kill you like Kramer, if you take one more step toward trying to contact this man Pabst.' He ended on a note of finality which suggested the matter was closed.

Simon was really angry now. He took a step nearer the chair, shot out a muscular arm and grabbed the top rail. He shook it – and Fragonard – rhythmically in a frenzy of rage. The Swiss was rattled about like a pea on a drum as Simon shouted, in time to his shaking, 'You – lousy – murderous – insulting – little – swine!! I'll do what I damn well like, you ponced-up old goat!'

He let the chair down with a bang and brought his face close to the other man's in defiance.

Fragonard was white with evil. After a pregnant moment of absolute silence, he spat straight in Simon's face.

Beside himself with disgust, the younger man returned the typically continental insult with a typically British one. He took a swinging punch at Fragonard's face and caught him at the side of the left eye. The smaller man was literally knocked sideways, off the chair and on to the floor. He staggered across the room and fetched up with a bang against the wardrobe.

Even as Simon fumbled for a handkerchief to wipe the spittle from his face, his anger cooled and he felt ashamed at having been so violent to a man twenty years older and half his size.

He need not have worried.

When he looked up over his handkerchief, the Swiss was facing him in a half-crouch, his face twisted with hate. He was clutching a small pistol and the little black hole in the end was looking Simon right in the eye.

Fragonard had a red flush around his eye already. His voice was breathless with passion. 'No one does that to Jules Fragonard ... I would kill you here and now, if it were not so – so inconvenient!' His words quivered with venom.

If Simon ever had any doubts that here was Kramer's assassin, they vanished now. He was a hair's breadth from the same fate at the hand of this psychopath.

His own anger collapsed into his boots. He stood deathly quiet, the handkerchief still at his lips.

He was afraid – a fear so acute that it seemed unreal. He had known almost the same feeling leading a platoon down a street in Nicosia, knowing that any second a sniper's bullet could smash him out of existence.

But this was no distant sniper – this was an enraged man, right there behind that little black hole. Simon stood paralysed.

Slowly, still crouching, Fragonard moved back to his chair and slid onto it, the rail against his chest. He held the automatic high, its snout poking over the top of the chair. His bald head, his little beard and the long woollen dressing gown should have been comic, but no one felt like laughing.

'You young fool!' he hissed, his voice tight with frustrated reprisal. 'If only I could teach you a lesson! ... but you so much as think of interfering in my arrangements and I will kill you with the greatest of pleasure!'

Simon slowly lowered the handkerchief. He was astounded and sickened by the change to hate and evil in the little man, who had become almost a figure of gentle fun over the past few days.

Fragonard was continuing his string of offensively framed orders.

'You will not write, telephone or contact this man Pabst in any way. You will do nothing except keep your nose clean and be a good little tourist ... confine yourself to tumbling girls on your bed and I might overlook your incredible stupidity this evening!'

Once more, the words, delivered in the most insulting way imaginable, spurred Simon's temper into action. His fear fell from him, especially as Fragonard's pistol had dropped during the speech. It was replaced by icy, calculating rage.

Fragonard began to speak again. 'Now get out and ...'

The words ended in a gargling cry as Simon's foot smashed up to land under the soft seat of the chair. He caught the other man off balance and tipped him clean over backwards.

Fragonard still had an iron grip on the gun and Simon lunged after him to tear it from his grasp, but it was unnecessary.

As the older man flew full-length across the carpet, his head hit the skirting board at the edge of the communicating door. There was a sickening crack and he lay still, the pistol falling from his limp fingers.

For an awful moment, Simon thought he was dead. The fact that, half a minute before, Fragonard had been within an ace of shooting him was forgotten.

He knelt by his side and was immensely relieved to hear a heavy snoring breath come from the stricken man.

Simon slipped his arms around Fragonard's chest and heaved him up against his own chest, lugging him to the bed. He laid him flat and was even more relieved to see him stir and moan a little.

His gaze fell on the pistol, now lying against the wall. At least he could get rid of that – then he would be comparatively safe from the murderous little man, as Russia was the last place on earth in which to replace illicit weapons.

He picked it up by the trigger guard, with the vague notion of avoiding fingerprints, then looked around for somewhere to dispose of it. There seemed no where suitable in the room – then his eyes fell on the bathroom.

He went in and stood on the thick, ancient seat of the lavatory. There was an old-fashioned cast-iron cistern level with his face. He prised up the cover, ignoring the trickles of rusty water that ran down his wrist, and dropped the automatic inside, well clear of the siphon.

Jumping down, he pulled the chain to make sure that the gun wasn't fouling the mechanism, then went quickly to the bedroom entrance. Fragonard was groaning loudly now and trying to push himself up on one elbow. His injury seemed to be much less serious that it had first appeared.

'There's more where that came from, chum;' growled Simon with a touch of bravado. He felt suddenly sick and longed for his bed. All the delayed effects of the evening's drinking and emotions rushed over him as he slipped out and shut the door behind him.

Chapter Seven

Simon awoke to a painful drumming in his head. At first, the thoughts that penetrated his hangover tried to convince him that it was only the pounding of blood in his tortured arteries, but gradually he was forced to accept that someone was actually pounding on his door.

Opening his eyes, he was momentarily surprised to find that he wasn't in his own Bayswater room. Then the fog cleared away sufficiently for him to grasp that he was in Moscow and that his watch showed five thirty; presumably a.m.?

The knocking again conveyed a sense of urgency through the door. Stumbling into his dressing gown, he tottered across the room, the journey seeming to take half a day. As he reached the little passage alongside the bathroom, he heard Elizabeth's voice.

'Simon, please, let me in!'

The hope that she had come to seduce him did not even flicker through his mind. Early morning and the events of the night before had chased any lust from his mind. Even when he opened the door and had the luscious brunette almost fall in on him, dressed only in a revealing black and pink negligee, his mood remained one of fuddled resentment.

'Liz – what the hell? It's only half five!'

His voice trailed away as he saw her face through his own red-rimmed eyes. She was dead white and without make-up, looked like a corpse.

'Didn't you hear the commotion … listen!' she quavered.

Her usual poise had gone. Fighting off the dark-brown feeling that threatened to engulf him, Simon heard something above the buzzing in his ears.

In the corridor, he could hear the muffled tramp of feet and men's voices.

'What's going on?' he muttered, but Liz had broken away and run to the window. Heedless of her revealing silhouette against the light, she threw open the two frames and leaned out. Immediately, the sounds of an engine revving, metallic scraping noises and voices shouting in Russian came up to the fourth floor.

Simon shuffled across, clutching his maroon robe about him in an apology to modesty.

Looking down – which gave him momentary nausea – he saw half a dozen figures apparently wrestling on the waste ground inside the Chinese Wall. From that height, they were curiously foreshortened and looked like Japanese dolls.

'They woke me up a few minutes ago!' gabbled Liz Treasure. 'Isn't it terrible, the poor man!' Her voice rose in a wail.

Simon rested his head in his hands and closed his eyes for a second.

'Isn't what terrible,' he asked dully, then leaned out again and refocused with an effort.

The lethargy left him as if iced water had been thrown in his face. The 'wrestlers' had parted and he saw that they had been struggling with a stretcher. Some of them were blue uniformed militia, the rest hotel staff. On the stretcher lay a still figure dressed in a vivid yellow outfit.

Simon swung around to Liz, who had been hovering behind him, trying to see over his shoulder.

'Who is it – what's happened?'

'Poor Monsieur Fragonard … he's dead!'

She wailed again and put her knuckles to her mouth.

Simon found time to compare her with the heroine of an old silent movie. Then he turned back to the window, his hangover forgotten.

The men below were carrying the stretcher across a few yards of barren, weed-strewn ground to a grey ambulance, which was providing the engine noises.

'How do you know it's him?' he called ungrammatically over his shoulder.

She leant on his back, trembling. He was momentarily conscious of the pressure of her soft body.

'Those lime-coloured pyjamas … they're his. I saw them when he opened his case at the Customs. And anyway, he's directly below his window … and he's dead!'

As her voice shrilled at the end, the fact of death was convincingly proved down below, as one of the militiamen took a blanket from the ambulance and spread it over the body, covering the face.

As they slid the stretcher into the back of the vehicle. Simon swung back into the room and took Elizabeth by the shoulders.

'You shouldn't have looked, dear … come and sit down.'

She looked at him with a sudden wildness. 'That's not it – it's the police I'm afraid of … they'll be all over us … they'll …'

She got no further as there was a violent rapping on the door and it was pushed open without more ado.

A thin, cadaverous-faced man stood there, dressed in an ill-fitting blue uniform with wide red epaulettes on the shoulders. He held a military-style cap in one hand.

Behind him hovered a bleary-faced, unshaven Gilbert, barefooted and dressed in an exotic kimono.

Liz Treasure gave a little squeal and hugged herself across her prominent bosom. She ran for the door, aware at last of the transparency of her outfit.

The eagle-faced officer raised a hand to stop her, but suddenly realized the reason for her flight and quickly looked away. She slipped past him and vanished at top speed, while Pudovkin addressed himself to Simon.

'Will you come out into the corridor, please?' he asked, speaking good English, but with a hesitancy that suggested that he had not used it for a long time.

Gilbert Bynge rose on tip-toe behind the speaker.

'Sorry, old chap, there's been a bit of a tragedy ... d'you mind rallying round?'

His twitch seems to have worsened, Simon thought irrelevantly. He put his legs into top gear with an effort and wearily went over to the door, stepping into his slippers en route.

'I saw it,' he said shortly, as he came up to the Soviet officer. He had seen both the militiaman and the courier opening their mouths to begin explanations and felt like getting in first.

Alexei Pudovkin snapped his shut, then opened it to spit out a question.

'You say you saw it?'

'I mean I saw what the trouble was ... Monsieur Fragonard, I think.'

Gilbert began babbling almost incoherently. Like Liz, he had lost his normal smoothness in the face of an emergency. 'Terrible ... terrible! Never had a trip like it before ... your Helsinki business, then this ... can't imagine what the Company will say about it ... the man must have been round the bend.'

Simon stared at Gilbert. 'You mean he jumped out of the window deliberately?' He had already assumed that the still, yellow body had fallen from the fourth floor.

The leathery detective officer threw his hands between them like a referee at a wrestling match.

'Please, please! Let us keep all talk for a moment. I wish for no discussion between persons yet.'

He said this quite politely, but there was an edge to his voice that allowed no misunderstanding.

They had edged their way out to the corridor and Simon saw that two militiamen were banging on other doors further down.

A young officer came out of Fragonard's room and stood attentively behind the captain, who turned to Simon and said, 'It is necessary that we all go at once to the sitting room at the head of the stairs to discuss this unfortunate occurrence.'

Gilbert looked at Simon and shrugged expressively. 'Sorry, old boy ... at the double, I'm afraid. Will you give Mrs Treasure a shout or shall I?'

Gilbert went to chivvy the parson, the two old ladies and Michael Shaw, whilst Simon called explanations through Liz's door. In a moment, she appeared elegantly dressed in a red brocade dressing gown over her décolletage. Even in that short time, she had fluffed up her hair and put on some emergency make-up.

As they began the long walk to the stair head, the vicar, the old ladies and Shaw appeared, to join in the procession that formed behind the militia lieutenant.

Michael Shaw looked an even worse mess than usual. His red hair and beard was tangled and his cheeks were grey with a hangover. He wore a shabby green dressing gown which was open to the waist, revealing a bare and hairy chest. The general appearance was that of a dissolute Robin Hood.

Several Russian guests had been rousted out of their rooms and they too joined the migration.

Simon looked over his shoulder at the silent cavalcade and was reminded all too keenly of tales of 'a knock in the night' in the bad old Stalin days.

He slid a hand under Elizabeth's elbow. 'Feel a bit like the aristos being carted off to the guillotine,' he whispered jocularly, hoping to raise a smile on the woman's face. To his alarm, her eyes opened wide with horror and she began to sob quietly into her handkerchief.

Terrified, he tried to undo his mistake. 'Come on, Liz,' he pleaded, 'Look, these coppers have to ask their questions, the same as our fellows. After all the poor chap *did* fall from his window – they'd have to make inquiries back in England, just the same. You know, "did he fall or was he pushed?" routine.'

He almost bit his tongue out as he said the words, as Elizabeth went off into worse paroxysms of silent weeping.

By the time they reached the last bend, her sobs had subsided to a snivel. 'But I'm so worried!' she sniffed. He squeezed her arm reassuringly, but frowned to himself. *What the devil does she mean by 'worried'?* Frightened, scared, perhaps – but 'worried' was a funny word to use.

He had his own worries.

What the hell happened to Fragonard after I left him last night? The evil little man seemed to be recovering all right – surely he couldn't have been so chagrined at his failure that he threw himself from the window! Ridiculous! So how did he fall?

He gave it up and concentrated on fighting off his hangover, which threatened to return now that the first shock was passing.

The procession had straggled into single file by the time they reached the lounge and Simon was reminded of a chain gang, minus the shackles, from the weary slouch and silence of the members.

The 'lounge' was the open space at the head of the staircase where the lift debouched and where the old lady sat guarding her keys at a small desk. Unlike Western hotels, where one leaves one's room key at the reception counter, in the Metropol each floor had a grim old woman who collected and dispensed them. Simon had heard it rumoured that another of her functions was to guard the morals of the floor and see that no one smuggled stray women to their room.

Behind this old dragon's desk was an open carpeted area, with a few sofas and chairs and a large television set, though Simon had yet to see any one actually use the place.

Perhaps they keep them for murders, he thought cynically.

'Please, will you all sit down?' Pudovkin had a deep, mellow voice, at odds with his cadaverous appearance.

'Do you want the rest of my party up here?' asked Gilbert, in English for the benefit of the others. Simon had carefully concealed the fact that he spoke Russian himself.

The militia officer shook his head. 'They are the other floor, I think – we will confine ourselves to this for now. Please sit,' he added rather testily, as no one had attempted to use the seats.

One by one, they slumped down, Simon steering Elizabeth to a red plush settee which looked as if it may have belonged the last-but-one Tsar.

The Russian guests still stood and looked uncertainly at the militia. Moiseyenko spoke to them and there began a rapid exchange between all the Russians, with much gesticulating.

'They're saying that they were all fast asleep and don't know anything about anything!' hissed Gilbert in a rapid, free translation, which Simon had already made for himself.

After this brief exchange, the native guests marched stiffly away with righteous expressions on their faces, leaving the detectives with seven Britishers. Two uniformed militiamen stood with their backs to the lift and the old woman sat rigidly at her desk, her back to the group in the lounge.

'I regret that interruption, but it was necessary to let the citizens go back to their rooms ... now!'

Pudovkin cleared his throat for action, then paused as an old-fashioned clock on the wall chimed six o'clock.

His heart sank.

This was the time that Darya and he normally got up. This morning he had been called at five because of this emergency and he had dashed off without taking a bundle of clothes that she had left for the dry-cleaner. She had spent half an hour putting them ready the previous evening and a further hour telling him what she would do to him if he forgot to take them – and he had!

Tonight would be unbearable when he got home ... he devoutly wished that this case would go for at least a week, without a break, so that she might have time to simmer down.

He pulled himself together with an effort, and addressed his audience.

'I am Detective Captain Pudovkin and this is my assistant, Lieutenant Moiseyenko,' he began solemnly. 'I apologise for my English which may not be so good, but it will be good enough for us to understand each other, I think.'

Elizabeth began to giggle surreptitiously and Simon wondered if his diagnosis of impending hysterics was going to come true. He doubted if he was capable of slapping her face.

Alexei appeared not to have noticed and went on with his build-up.

'You must all know by now that unfortunately one of your fellow-travellers, Monsieur Fragonard, has met with his death by dropping from his window. The distance was great ...'

'Twenty metres – more than sixty of your feet,' interposed Moiseyenko solemnly.

'He had severe injuries, as expected,' went on Pudovkin. 'Our medical service, which attended as soon as possible, was unable to do anything for him. He was quite dead when found on the floor.'

There was a gurgled murmur of understanding from the group.

'So now we must find out all we can.'

He cleared his throat again.

'I would like to hear from each of you if you heard or saw anything during the night … firstly, taking the rooms next to Fragonard. Mrs Treasure, I think you are in Room 514?'

Liz's arm jerked nervously beneath Simon's hand. He felt her start to tremble as she sat bolt upright.

'Take it easy, sweet,' he murmured, 'He's not going to bite you!'

Pudovkin paused to pull a wad of passports from the side pocket of his jacket. As he sorted through them to find Elizabeth's, Simon wondered how he had got hold of them so quickly, as neither the hotel bureau nor the Intourist office would be open for another couple of hours.

The detective studied the passport, but made no reference to it when he spoke. 'Did you hear anything unusual during the night … or was there anything about the dead man last evening that was …' he struggled for a word, 'was unique?'

Even as he said it, he winced. It was the wrong word, but he was immediately distracted by seeing Elizabeth Treasure looking fleetingly but uneasily at the man Smith.

'Well – was there?' he barked, his eyes flickering between the two of them. Liz coloured up 'No – no. Only last night, we were all a little confused. We had a party,' she ended lamely.

Simon breathed again. For a moment, he thought she was going to say that he had gone off to Fragonard's room almost at midnight … though she still may have let the cat out of the bag. This Russian Sherlock Holmes must have seen the guilty look she gave him.

83

He suddenly found that Pudovkin was speaking to him.

'And you, Mr Smith … what about you?'

The Soviet militia captain was standing now with his hands behind his back, his head stuck out inquiringly like an old crow on a garden fence.

'Me – no, I heard nothing. Sorry, but we were all a bit drunk last night – weren't we, Gilbert?' He grinned glassily across at the courier, who jumped into life like a puppet on a string.

'Oh, rather … had a bit of a revel anyway, all of us. Slept like a log myself, until this morning – terrible business; don't know what I'll tell the Company!'

Pudovkin came relentlessly back to Simon.

'What time did you go to bed?'

'Ah, I'm not really sure – about eleven thirty, I think. Mrs Treasure was with me,' he added thoughtlessly.

Alexei's eyebrows climbed his forehead.

'In bed?' he asked primly.

Moiseyenko looked shocked. The young communist puritan in him was offended by the readiness with which the Westerners admitted it.

Simon stuttered out his explanations. 'No, no – in my room!'

The fact that Liz had *virtually* been in bed with him made it all the more difficult to deny. 'I mean, she called into my room for a last drink before she went to bed – that's what I mean.'

Pudovkin breathed out heavily through his long nose. 'And you saw and heard nothing later – nor left your room?'

Simon shook his head mutely, afraid to put his foot in it again. Pudovkin turned to Michael Shaw, who was slumped there like a great zombie. His long body was jack-knifed into an ancient armchair that might have been new when Lenin was a boy.

Shaw's face had got a little colour back, but his eyes still looked like footprints in the snow.

The detective captain shuffled the passports about until he came to one which carried a portrait of a more respectable bearded man.

'You are Mr Michael Shaw from the Republic of Ireland?' he asked severely, but with perfect politeness.

Shaw's head rose and the red fronds around his mouth parted.

'I am that.'

His brogue was deliberately overdone, but whether from patriotism or by way of insult, no one could tell.

'Are you staying in Room 516?'

This rated only a tired nod.

'The one next to the dead man's room?'

Another jerk of the head.

'With a communicating door.'

A statement, not a question and it brought a flash of Celtic temper to Shaw's face. 'Sure, and there's a damned great lump of furniture against it and all!'

He scowled ferociously at Pudovkin, who held up a hand 'I was going to ask only if you heard anything in the night – a door is more transparent to sound than a wall.'

Another mistake, that 'transparent', he thought, chiding himself.

Shaw shook his head, apparently mollified. 'Devil a thing – I was paralytic all night.'

Alexei frowned until he worked out the big man's meaning.

'When did you see Fragonard last?'

'God, who knows the time in a place like this! ... he went from the restaurant before me – I stayed until no one would give me any more liquor. About half past eleven or thereabouts, I guess.'

His brown eyes rolled a little, showing bloodshot whites at the corners. He scrabbled at the open neck of his dressing gown to hide his chest, which was almost as hairy as his face.

After a few words with the terrified parson and with the two old ladies who seemed half-deaf and half-daft with fright, Pudovkin had a murmured consultation with Moiseyenko, who had written down all that was said. He turned back to the group. 'Thank you, I have no more questions for the moment, as certain investigations now have to be carried out.'

He cleared his throat and spoke to Gilbert Bynge.

'I see no reason why you should not continue your tour activities until further notice – what do you do today?'

Gilbert shot nervously to his feet, like a small boy before his teacher.

'We were – are – going to the Tretyakov Art Gallery this afternoon. This morning was free for shopping or personal activities.'

Pudovkin scratched his bristly chin. 'Then I would like to see you all here again at one o'clock today, please.' With a curt nod, he turned and clumped to the head of the stairs, followed by his lieutenant and the stolid militiamen.

Deflated by anti-climax, the tourists began the long haul back to their rooms at the other end of the cavernous passage.

The clergyman and the twittering old ladies, bound by a mutual bond of incomprehension, lagged behind, the younger ones trudging ahead in sour silence.

Shaw broke the ice at the first bend. 'Not seven o'clock yet, and here's me on me bloody feet already!' he growled, shuffling along in a cheap pair of Hong Kong 'flip-flop' slippers. 'I should be asking for me money back – some damn holiday this is turning out.'

Gilbert, mouth twitching more than ever, ran a desperate hand through his straw-like hair. His receding chin quivered and, for a moment, Simon thought he was going to cry.

'It's awful – awful … I'll have to telegraph London Office as soon as the bureau opens. They'll have to notify his family or someone.'

He launched into a hand-wringing monologue of self-pity in which 'London Office' was repeated over and over like some holy creed.

When they reached the end of the corridor, the other men slunk off to their own rooms with a muttered 'See you at breakfast.'

Simon hustled Elizabeth Treasure into his own room and shut the door. She had sniffed her way in silence from the lounge and he was dying to consolidate the alibi she had given him.

He kissed her rather hastily on the cheek.

'Thanks for saying what you did, darling.'

She looked at him with big searching eyes. He had never seen them before without their false lashes and elaborate fortifications of mascara, but they were still very attractive.

'I don't know why I did, really,' she murmured. 'It isn't as if he's been murdered or anything, is it?'

He put an arm around her shoulders and squeezed her.

'Of course not … I can't understand what happened to the old boy … did he commit suicide or just fall from the damn window? We'd all had a drop of the vodka, but none of us was tiddly enough to go falling from windows!'

They sat on the edge of the bed and Simon took her hand.

'What did he want, when he came here last night?' she asked.

Simon had been waiting for this. He furiously beat his brains for some reasonable excuse – what came out was no gem of inspiration.

'Writing – we'd been talking on the boat about it.'

'At midnight, after a beat-up like that meal?' she said incredulously.

He shrugged. 'He was a funny bloke – but had some publishing connections in Geneva. I've been thinking about writing a book about Cyprus.'

She sniffed again – he wasn't sure whether it was a head cold or just plain disbelief. 'You never mentioned it before – and why would the Swiss be interested in a book about the British Army ... and who was that Kramer he mentioned?'

Simon cursed inwardly as he got deeper into the mire. 'Kramer – oh, he's a literary agent in London.'

Elizabeth was silent for a moment. 'So there was no need, really, for me to tell lies to the police just now?'

He squeezed her hand in panic. 'Yes ... it saved such a lot of trouble; you know, all that "you were the last person to see the dead man alive" business. They would pester the life out of me, and all for nothing ... Fragonard was alive and kicking when I left him.'

Alive maybe, but certainly not kicking. The doubts that he really was responsible for the death of the fat man kept floating across Simon's mind. *Had* that crack on the head from the skirting board confused Fragonard so much that he'd later staggered blindly about the room and fallen out of the window – perhaps whilst trying to get some air?

Simon looked at his own window again and was reassured by the height and width of the sill. But suicide seemed out of the question – an aggressive psychopathic killer would be ready to take other lives, but certainly not his own.

Liz suddenly got up. 'I must go and put some clothes on – God, I feel awful. Must look a sight too.'

She stood up and swayed a little. Simon rose and kissed her, but her response was listless.

'Not at my passionate best, sweetie,' she murmured and tottered away to put on a face for the day.

Simon lay on the bed when she had gone.

He clasped his hands behind his head and stared at the ornate cornices of the ceiling. He thanked his lucky stars that he had thought of dumping Fragonard's pistol in the 'loo' – as long as some nosey militiaman didn't find it.

It slowly dawned on him that not only the gun, but Fragonard himself was permanently out of the way.

His threats about Simon keeping clear of Gustav Pabst no longer held any meaning. As long as this accident didn't stir the militia up into too much curiosity, a quick bit of footwork would clear the whole matter up inside a few hours.

Simon fumbled for a cigarette and lay back to inhale with satisfaction. For the first time, something had at last gone in his favour.

Chapter Eight

'Where have they taken the body, Vasily?'

'To the Sechenov First Moscow Institute of Medicine – the mortuary of the City Service is out of commission – laying new drains or something'

'The Sechenov First ... that's down Pirogovskaya way, isn't it?' grunted Pudovkin.

'Yes – a bit this side of the Lenin Stadium.'

Most of Vasily's landmarks had some connection with sport. Both the great football arena and one of the medical colleges were down in the south-west part of the city, in the district formed by a great bend in the Moskva River.

The two detectives were sitting in the main CID room of Petrovka. It was twenty past seven and only two of the night staff and a couple of cleaners were in the big office.

Pudovkin ran a bony hand through his hair. 'I'd better speak to the Old Man about the autopsy.' He reached for a phone and dialled Colonel Mitin's home number, whilst Moiseyenko wandered off to refill their cups from the communal coffee pot on its gas ring near the door. While he waited for his chief to finish speaking to the commissioner, he looked around the big room that was the focal point of his life as a detective. The steel filing cabinets around the walls, the untidy, busy desks, the papers and folders, the faded maps on the walls, noticeboards with half-forgotten standing orders, dog-eared reference books and well-thumbed copies of the Criminal Code ... all these were as familiar as the inside of his bachelor room at the militia hostel. He had no way of

91

knowing it, but he was looking at a replica of almost any CID office in the world.

Alexei dropped the phone and Vasily hurried over to him.

'Our Fat Father agreed with me,' announced Pudovkin, sounding satisfied. 'He thinks this is a case with a difference, so we'll play it carefully. I'd never forgive myself if those vultures from The Centre[6] took it over and found holes to pick in our work.'

'So what do we do now?'

Vasily reminded the older man of a sprinter waiting for the gun.

'I'm treating it as a murder until proved otherwise –all this business with Smith … a very special murder too. So I'm asking the Forensic Research Institute to do the autopsy.'

Alexei got up from the borrowed desk and rubbed his hands in suppressed excitement. 'Come into my office and bring your book – we've got some organising to do.' A fleeting vision of Darya and the bag of laundry passed through his mind, but he threw it out. He promised himself then that he would get a divorce, even if he had to sell his precious cameras and fishing tackle to help raise the money.

They went through into Alexei's cubicle and while Vasily frowned at the untidy jumble in his notebook, Alexei dialled another phone number. The conversation was short and apparently satisfactory, as Pudovkin was actually grinning when he put the receiver down. His ulcer seemed to have undergone a miraculous cure.

'Going like clockwork, Vasily Sergeyevich!'

Moiseyenko pointed at the phone. 'I thought the Research place didn't do routine work – only high-powered consultative stuff?'

---

[6]Muscovites' nickname for the KGB headquarters.

His captain nodded. 'Usually so, yes – but if they're asked from high enough up – like our Commissioner – they'll oblige.'

Alexei and his assistant spent a few minutes making administrative arrangements about this and some other current cases, so that the day ahead would show some semblance of order and routine. Then Pudovkin got up and rubbed his eyes, which still carried early morning sleep.

'Come on, let's get back to the Metropol and see how the Incident Squad are making out ... I said we'd be at the autopsy room by nine.'

They walked the few blocks to the hotel and called in on the manager before going up to the fourth floor.

The poor man was grey with worry ... a death under any circumstances was bad enough, but the suspicious death of a foreigner already under double surveillance was ten times worse. He wondered what fate had sent him here instead of to the Ukraina or the National across the square.

'Are you going to arrest them all and take them out of here?' he asked hopefully.

Alexei's cheeks crinkled like old leather. 'All of them, *tovarishch*? D'you think they set on this man like a pack of wolves and tossed him out of your window, eh?' He stopped grinning. 'Now, who was on floor duty at the desk before that old woman Elena Anokhina ... I've already spoken to her.'

The manager churned through a pile of papers on his desk and turned up two names.

'Have them here at noon, I want to see if either of them heard or saw anything during last evening on the fourth floor ... and I'll be sending another woman detective around this afternoon, so give her a uniform and a brush and let her hang around as a chambermaid.'

They went on up to Room 514, leaving the manager wishing that he had never left Voronezh.

The corridor outside the room was awash with detectives and technicians. The door of the bedroom was covered in grey fingerprint powder and a man with a large camera on a tripod was in a foul temper, cursing as people kept passing in front of his lens.

Inside, another photographer had just finished and was packing up his kit. Another pair of laboratory men were crawling about the floor, putting wisps of fluff into cellophane packets.

A thickset lieutenant, almost as old as Pudovkin, came across to meet them. He was the Incident Squad leader, in charge of the organised chaos that was going on around them.

'See here, comrade captain, along the wall and skirting board.' He pointed to the high fascia board running along the base of the wall adjacent to Michael Shaw's room. On the blue emulsion paint of the wall as well as on the varnish of the wood, there were some splattered brownish stains, quite small, but numerous.

'Blood all right – and quite fresh – the colour is due to the stuff it's landed on.'

Alexei looked at the communicating door and the blood spots for a moment, then walked to the open window. He looked out and saw the Chinese Wall curving towards the hotel slightly to his left.

'There's something on the sill, captain.' The squad leader pointed to some fresh scratches on the white-painted wood. They passed right across its width, reaching the outer glazing frame.

'They're black – look like toe drag-marks from a pair of shoes,' observed Pudovkin.

The lieutenant nodded. 'I thought so, too – I'll get the whole board cut out and sent to the laboratory.'

Alexei turned around and looked at the room again. 'Anything else?' Several men shook their heads.

'What about his luggage?'

'Nothing obvious … fancy shirts and a couple of suits. A camera and a couple of decadent picture magazines – all fast cars and half-dressed women.'

'Send the camera to have the film developed, just in case'

Pudovkin made his way to the door, with Moiseyenko in close pursuit.

'What do you think about it, *tovarishch* captain?' asked the squad man.

'I don't think anything until we've got some facts … but if you jump from a window, you shouldn't leave toe marks across the sill … and when you hit the ground, your blood shouldn't spurt up four floors and come in through the window, eh?'

He motioned to Moiseyenko and they made their way down to the rear of the hotel, through the passage Simon Smith had used the previous day, to emerge on the waste ground. A militia patrolman was standing watch over a chalk mark on the hard earth about four metres from the wall of the hotel. He saluted as they came up.

Alexei looked at the ground, then up at the cliff-face of the Metropol, pierced by rows of windows.

'Slightly off to one side – that's 515 up there,' Vasily pointed to the head of one of the Incident Squad which was poking through a window. It was hastily pulled back.

Pudovkin looked down again at the mute, but expressive chalk mark.

'He couldn't have drifted this far during the fall unless he bounced.'

They searched the surrounding area and it soon became clear that Fragonard had hit the ground a few feet nearer the wall than his body's final resting place. There was a dent in the ground and some weeds were crushed in the hollow.

'No blood anywhere, in spite of that upstairs,' said Alexei thoughtfully.

'One of the men upstairs said he had a cut on the back of his head – he saw it when they were putting the body in the ambulance.'

Vasily was enjoying playing Watson to Pudovkin's Holmes – that was one of the Western books that Moiseyenko really enjoyed, in spite of all the aristocrats and humble servants that filled the pages. The detective captain soon gave up his bloodhound act and set off back to the hotel.

'We'll see what the man from the Institute has to say about the injuries.'

Leaving the militiaman standing like a statue in his long blue overcoat, they walked back to Petrovka 38 to get a car to take them down to Pirogovskaya.

They were just driving out of the transport pool in another black Volga when a clerk ran breathlessly down from the duty room to hand a small parcel through the window. 'Just arrived on an early flight from Leningrad, from Militia HQ.'

As they drove off into the morning rush hour, Alexei unwrapped a shoebox, inside which nestled a small automatic pistol wrapped in yesterday's *Pravda*.

A sheet of paper with the Leningrad Militia heading lay underneath, but it told them nothing except that this was the gun found in Simon's cabin aboard the *Yuri Dolgorukiy*.

'I can't see what use it is having this,' muttered Alexei 'It hasn't been used – it wasn't even brought into the country.'

He slowly repacked the pistol into its box.

'Still, I'll bet a year's pension that this turns out to be murder.'

'Unless we're unlucky and the pathologists tell us it was a suicide or an accident.' Moiseyenko sounded afraid that he might be right.

Alexei poured scorn on the idea. 'I believe in coincidences like that as much as I believe in fairies, Vasily Sergeivich! Fragonard was flung from that window by someone and hit the ground with a fatal attack of gravitational force!'

Which only goes to show that even experienced detective captains can occasionally be wrong.

The militia car sped down Bolshaya Pirogovskaya Street and, just past the Air Ministry building, turned sharp right and stopped outside a small, old building set in some trees. This was the Pathology department of the Sechenov First Moscow Institute of Medicine, and combined the forensic medicine department under the same roof. A burly, genial man in his fifties met them on the steps.

'Back to the "temple of truth", eh, Alexei Alexandrovich?'

He thumped Pudovkin on the shoulder, nearly knocking his lean body to the ground.

The captain introduced him to Moiseyenko as they went into the gloomy entrance. The two senior men were old friends, it seemed.

'We had plenty of work together when I was in the City Service,' boomed the doctor, whose name was Gyenka Segel. 'Now I'm a damned armchair pathologist. This will be an excuse for keeping away from the paperwork for a couple of hours!'

Inside the main doors, it seemed half-dark and the place stank of varnish and embalming fluid.

'This way, to the left – the next performance is just about to begin!'

The exuberant Segel guffawed and treated Moiseyenko to one of his karate-like backslaps. Opening a door, he stood back to let them through. As they went down a couple of steps onto a terrazzo floor, the sickly-sweet smell of death flooded over the two militiamen.

Pudovkin had experienced it many times, but familiarity brought no relief. Vasily had paid about a dozen visits to autopsies, but this large teaching institute looked at first sight like something from an illustrated copy of Dante's *Inferno*.

Dr Segel boomed in his ear and he braced himself for another blow between the shoulder blades. 'Try these for size, comrades.'

Caps and gowns were produced from a side table and as they stood fumbling them on, the lieutenant stared around the autopsy room. An old, high-vaulted place, it contained five porcelain tables, around four of which clustered gowned doctors and students, like ants over a dead beetle.

Naked electric bulbs hung on long wires from the ceiling, and as the students milled around for a better view, he kept getting glimpses of flesh and bones, glinting horribly red in the harsh light. There was a buzz of discussion at each table, the pathologists teaching and the students asking questions.

'Your customer is over here.' Gyenka Segel marched off across the hall to the deserted table, his bald head gleaming under the lamps. They followed him, slopping through water patches stained ominously pink near the tables.

A white-gowned woman broke away from one group and joined them as they reached Segel.

'This is Dr Evdokia Yashina,' he said, with a gesture at the thick-set woman. 'She is a senior member of the staff here and will assist me.'

Comrade Yashina nodded abruptly at them, a forbidding figure in a rubber apron and thick gloves.

An attendant brought Gyenka the same things and, as he stood pulling the gloves over his great hairy fingers, another assistant removed a sheet from the still shape on the table.

'Let's get this straight again, Alexei ... this fellow fell from the fourth floor of the Metropol sometime during the night?'

Pudovkin re-told the whole story as fully as he knew it and ended, 'The Procurator's Office said just now that they don't intend to take it over straight away, so we have to follow it up until told to keep off.'

Segel scowled. 'Not like them to pass the buck so readily – I wonder if they've been tipped off from higher up?'

Alexei shrugged. 'I'm not complaining – we'll hang on to it as long as we can. There's no sign that the Dzerzhinsky Street mob are involved.'

Segel moved forward and stared impassively at the body. His assistant stood grimly on the other side of the table, her hands folded over her ample stomach.

There was another cloth over the face of the corpse and Segel whipped it off with a flourish that would have done credit to a conjurer unveiling a cage of white rabbits.

He smiled down at the calm features of the battered Jules Honore Fragonard.

'Pyjamas and a slipper on the left foot – and dressing gown.'

Alexei grunted. 'The other slipper was found at the foot of the wall outside – there were scratches across the windowsill that could have been made by black leather like this. The Criminalistics Laboratory are going to compare the polish stains.'

One of the attendants stood dutifully alongside, taking notes on a clipboard when Segel or the woman threw comments at him. The senior pathologist bent over the body again and poked at the bright yellow-green pyjamas.

'The front of the trouser legs are torn – bits of earth and weeds inside. Abrasions of the face and hands, with dirt in the wounds.'

He looked up at Pudovkin. 'Any blood on the ground where he fell?' His bantering humour fell away when he was actually at work.

Alexei looked at Moiseyenko, who was trying to keep his stomach in the right place.

'What would you say, Vasily ... very little, eh?'

The lieutenant gulped and nodded rapidly. 'Hardly any – it was bare earth, but I saw no more than a few spots.'

The burly pathologist had a muttered conference with the woman, then turned back to the detectives.

'I don't understand it, to tell the truth. Under these rips in the trousers, there are great gashes in the legs. They should have poured blood, but as you see, there's only a local staining of the cloth – ghastly stuff that it is,' he added, fingering the lime-coloured material with distaste. 'You agree, Evdokia Maximova?'

The hard-faced female glared at the body for a full quarter-minute before replying. 'Yes, I agree, but I want to see the insides before passing any more opinions ... and why the bruise around the eye – that's one thing, and this staining around the cut on the head is another.'

Segel skipped around to the top of the porcelain slab to look at the head of the victim. He sucked in his breath mightily and stood back with Evdokia to stare at the corpse, as if challenging Fragonard to explain himself.

'Why indeed!' hissed Gyenka Segel dramatically.

An hour later, the quartet sat in a tiny office, drinking a hot, dark fluid optimistically called instant coffee. Segel had a wad of handwritten notes in front of him, the fruit of their recent labours in the post-mortem room.

'Murder, Alexei Alexandrovich ... murder, definite murder!' He sounded as if he was trying to set the words to music.

'All these things add up to something very odd ... I don't pretend to know exactly what, but I can assure you that this man Fragonard was dead before he hit the ground ... he had severe injuries, mainly to his pelvis and legs, but he was dead before they happened.'

Alexei scowled up at him from his chair. 'But the bruised eye and the cut on the top of the head were done before death.'

Gyenka beamed back at him. 'Right ... there was considerable bleeding into the tissues of the eye and under the scalp – but the main feature about the head wound was that iodine had been dabbed on to it – and a dead man doesn't do that!'

'There was a bottle of iodine with his toilet things in the bathroom,' cut in Vasily, with some pride.

Alexei nodded at him – *this is the ability to observe that will take Moiseyenko to a Colonel's rank one day*, he thought.

He looked back at the extrovert Segel, who was perched on the edge of a table, sipping his steaming coffee.

'So if his main injuries were after death and his head injuries trivial, as you said earlier – what killed him?' demanded the detective.

Gyenka peered impishly at the grim Evdokia before answering. 'Ha – you hear that, citizeness? ... this is what the Western radio calls the "sixty-four million dollar question"! Shall I tell them or will you?'

She waved her permission with a stern hand and he went on happily.

'We know he didn't die from the main injuries caused in the fall, because there was almost no bleeding from them – the liver was torn, and the main artery at the back of the left knee was severed, but there was hardly any blood on the ground, you say. If he had been alive when it was torn, the haemorrhage would have been like the fountains in Ostankino Park!'

Moiseyenko heard this revolting simile with a return of his queasiness. His coffee turned sour in his mouth as Gyenka carried on with his oration with every sign of delight.

'His fractured pelvis, ribs and internal organs also showed no significant bleeding, so his heart must have been stopped when he fell.'

Alexei gestured impatiently. 'You keep telling us this – but what *actually* killed him?'

'Ah – I was keeping the best bit until last – I have never seen this method of killing in peacetime before. He was given a very sharp blow to the side of the neck, such as the traditional Japanese fighters use. The same thing is taught to our combat troops – and probably to those of every other army. The signs are slight, but distinct.'

'Such as …?' persisted Pudovkin.

'Bruising on the side of the neck and in the neck muscles. But, most convincing of all is the cracking of the cartilage of the voice box.'

Alexei scribbled some notes onto his pad, then grunted, 'Would this be a rapid death?'

Segel threw up his hands in mock drama. 'But yes! … instantly! The heart stops dead, which is the whole point in unarmed combat.'

Moiseyenko was listening intently, his nausea under control again.

'You said there were small bruises on the upper part of the arms and on the chest – very recent, like the eye … what about those?'

The pathologist shrugged and turned up his palms appealingly. 'Here even the great Segel is confounded … I don't know. I should think they were caused by knuckle blows.'

There was a momentary silence as each thought their private thoughts. Then Pudovkin asked his final question. 'And what about the time of death – can you now get any nearer than the service doctor who came to see the body on the ground?'

Segel gave another of his Parisian shrugs. 'Not really – you know from our past cases that fixing the time of death is most unreliable. We know he was dead just after five o'clock and from the high body temperature, it seems unlikely that he died before, say, three a.m. – possibly an hour later.'

'But certainly not late last night or around midnight?' Alexei seemed intent on pinning down the rather vague answer.

'Definitely not midnight ... even with all our inaccuracies, it couldn't have been before two o'clock.'

With this, the detectives had to be satisfied and they got up to leave.

'Telephone me just before noon, I may have something more for you then ... I'll be back at the Sadovaya Triumfalnaya.'

Their minds seething with the implications of Segel's conclusions, Pudovkin and Moiseyenko set out for Petrovka again.

Chapter Nine

In spite of his early morning hangover, Simon managed a good breakfast and felt all the better for it. A very pale Liz Treasure sat with him in the restaurant, picking at some rolls and drinking strong coffee.

They talked the affair over and over, getting exactly nowhere. It seemed to Simon that Liz seemed far more worried about the intentions of the militia than over the death of Fragonard. He recalled the curious thing she had said the previous evening ... something about not being a tourist, but on 'secret business'. *Silly idiot, probably the effects of the vodka*, he thought. He ladled butter onto another slice of rye bread and dismissed it from his overcrowded mind – he had troubles enough of his own.

Gilbert was eating at another table with the old ladies, trying to convince them that they were unlikely to end their tour in Lubyanka, the KGB prison only a stone's throw away from the Metropol. The courier looked pretty seedy himself. *Probably still trying to word that cable to 'Head Office'*, thought Simon.

There was no sign of Michael Shaw, though that was routine at this time of day – he was presumably breakfasting off a new bottle of Johnnie Walker in his bedroom.

The rest of the Trans-Europa tour were scattered about the restaurant, excitedly discussing the dramatic reduction in their number, but otherwise, life in the Metropol seemed to go on as usual.

'I'm going shopping this morning – we don't have to go to this art place till two, do we?' asked Liz at the end of the meal.

'No … do you mind if I don't come with you – I hate bloody shops and I've got a few things to do.'

She agreed with a readiness that rather puzzled him – in fact it seemed that if he wanted to go with her, she was ready to give him the brush-off again. He chalked up another question mark in his mind against the delectable but mysterious Mrs Treasure.

He made his way to the foyer and stood idly looking at the books and postcards at the newspaper stall. As he looked at some souvenirs displayed in a case behind the counter, he caught sight of a face mirrored in the glass. It was staring intently at him from over a newspaper, but as Simon turned around, the paper was hurriedly hoisted up in front of the man's eyes. He was a stocky fellow, dressed in a blue plastic raincoat and sat at the back of the foyer with his legs behind a small table. Simon had the idea that he had seen the same chap there the previous evening, but couldn't be sure.

There were a dozen other loungers in the foyer and another score milling up and down the steps from the entrance. Simon reasoned that half the Russian population were burly and short-necked and wore plastic mackintoshes, but the uneasiness remained. He began the trek back to his room in a thoughtful frame of mind. In the lift, he went over the mystery of Fragonard's death again, still worried that he himself might be the cause of the man's fatal fall.

There was something odd about his body … he had realized that when he looked from the window earlier on, but couldn't pin it down then. Now it came to him – pyjamas! Fragonard had been wearing a silver-grey suit beneath his dressing gown when Simon had left him last night – yet he died in those awful lime-green things! So

106

surely the crack on the head couldn't have been all that bad if the Swiss had been able to change his clothes.

He felt relieved that this helped to salve his conscience – even though Fragonard was a killer and had damned nearly shot Simon himself, he had no wish to be a self-appointed executioner.

He got to his room, looked at his wristwatch and began pacing up and down, uneasy about the man in the foyer. Going to the desk, he took out his map of Moscow, including the plan of the Metro system. He spent a few moments concentrating on the layout of certain streets and stations.

Satisfied with his homework at last, he put on his raincoat and slogged back to the foyer. He bought a copy of the *Morning Star* at the news-stand and saw that 'Blue Coat' was carefully taking no notice of him.

Leaving the hotel, he crossed the square and made for Gorky Street, the main thoroughfare of Moscow. He walked up the right-hand pavement for a while, ambling along past the shops and offices, trying to confirm the suspicion he had about the man in the foyer.

Hurrying crowds surged past him in both directions, men in uniform, pretty girls in high heels, old grannies in black headscarves and hundreds of ordinary citizens, half of them in blue plastic raincoats. Though he looked surreptitiously behind a few times, it was impossible to make out his own 'friend' in the crowd.

Simon turned off the pavement as soon as he could; a small park had been built around an equestrian statue and he saw a vacant place in the benches around the edge.

He squeezed between an old *babushka* rocking a baby in a perambulator and an equally old man dozing with a translation of *Hamlet* across his knee.

In a moment, he saw the burly man from the corner of his eye. He arrived at the street side of the park and stood hesitantly looking around, trying not to notice Simon.

107

There were no other empty seats and he began walking aimlessly up and down the other side of the park, looking for a place to sit.

Simon pulled out his *Morning Star*, the only English paper on sale at the hotel, and pretended to read, much to the undisguised interest of the grandmother on his left.

His eyes strayed above the page to watch Blue Coat. He had worked himself around the square and was waiting to jump into a vacant space that a woman seemed about to leave.

Simon wanted to keep him in sight all the time, but was suddenly distracted. A bony elbow dug him in the ribs.

'They're going to take it down, you know!'

He turned in surprise to see the face of the old woman looking up at him like a wrinkled prune. Her dark eyes twinkled, looking about a hundred years younger than the rest of her face.

'Take what down, mother?' he asked in Russian.

She took a skinny hand from the pram handle and pointed up at the armoured horseman on its plinth. 'Him ... Yuri Dolgorukiy. They're going to take him away and put another Yuri in his place.'

In spite of his preoccupation, the name rang a bell. As well as being the name of the ship where all the trouble began, it was the name of the founder of Moscow in the twelfth century. By some useless quirk of memory, Simon recalled that Yuri was the grandson of King Harold who lost the Battle of Hastings!

The old woman cackled and gave him another jab in the loin. 'Ay ... Gagarin, of course. Horses are out of date now, it's *sputniks* people want!'

Simon smiled at her, and made some comment in colloquial Russian, then turned his eyes back to his watcher.

He was nowhere to be seen. The vacant seat had been taken by another woman and of Blue Coat there was no sign.

Simon cursed under his breath at his own inattention, and hurried back to Gorky Street and along the pavement again.

A little way further on, he came to another little open space, this time with a monument to Pushkin. He sat down again here and waited. It was no good trying to dodge a chap if you didn't know where he was, he reasoned. He took a bench facing the street, with the *Izvestia* offices on his right and an ultra-modern cinema behind him. Sure enough, within a minute, the heavy-footed 'tail' appeared on the pavement. This time he walked straight past, but Simon knew full well that he had been noticed.

He chewed his lip anxiously. He had to throw this fellow off in such a way that it would look accidental – any deliberate evasion would draw immediate suspicion on himself.

He thought deeply for a moment, joining Pushkin in his attitude of profound contemplation. *Why am I being followed?* he ruminated. He optimistically hoped that all the fourth floor members of Trans-Europa were getting the same treatment and that he was not singled out for special attention.

An idea came eventually and, with a little prayer for success, he got up once more. 'May as well try it – nothing lost if it doesn't work,' he said aloud to the consternation of a passing Armenian in a little round hat.

Simon crossed Gorky Street at a set of pedestrian lights; his shadow dutifully waited for a second change of lights before following and Simon obligingly slowed down so that he wouldn't lose the man, before continuing to the Mayakovskaya Metro station. Blue Coat followed at a respectable distance as he went through the 'magic eye' barrier and down to the ornate palace underground.

There were quite a few people on the southbound platform which went back to the city centre. Simon moved in among the thickest patch and stopped behind a group of Vietnamese students. He noticed that his 'tail' had stopped exactly one car's length away so that he would be able to enter the same carriage through a different door.

A few seconds later, a train rushed in behind a wave of compressed air, looking almost identical to any train on London's Central Line. The doors opened with exactly the same 'pssst' and the Asian students jabbered their way inside the car.

Simon followed more slowly, noting that his shadow was waiting until the last moment, to make sure that Simon really did get on the train. He climbed in and saw that the other man followed suit at the other end of the car.

Deliberately, Simon stared down the central aisle and the thinly disguised militiaman hurriedly made his way to a seat to make himself less conspicuous.

Simon timed things perfectly.

He remained standing near the door, but looked around as if choosing a seat in the half-full carriage.

His ears were tuned for the platform guard shouting 'Mind the doors'. As soon as it came, he gave a rapid but convincing pantomime of patting his pockets in alarm, then as the doors were actually sliding shut, he leapt sideways through them as they hissed together inches behind him.

Outside on the platform, he continued his charade of furiously turning out his pockets in a futile search for his wallet.

The train was already accelerating rapidly, having started with a jerk as the doors slammed shut. He saw with relish that the betrayed sleuth had hurled himself from his seat to the doors, but by now the train was doing twenty miles an hour. A few seconds later, the car had flashed into the tunnel at the end of the platform, carrying the frustrated militiaman with it. Simon sighed with relief, stopped fishing in his pockets and walked to the opposite edge of the platform to catch the next northbound train in the opposite direction to the enraged follower.

He travelled to the next stop, Byelorusskiy, and changed again to begin the longer circle route to Gorky Park Station.

At eleven twenty, the phone rang in Pudovkin's office. He was outside in the main CID room, holding his cup under the spout of the coffee pot, and Moiseyenko answered it for him.

'It's Lev Pomansky – sounds as if he's in trouble again. Wants to speak to you,' he reported sardonically.

Alexei came to the phone and listened. A scowl passed over his face, then he sighed. 'All right, get back to the Metropol and watch for his coming back – do you think it was deliberate or genuine?' He listened for a few more seconds, then dropped the phone back with a grunt of annoyance.

'What's he done this time?' asked Vasily.

'Lost the Smith fellow – on the Metro!'

Vasily whistled. 'He gave him the slip?'

Pudovkin shrugged and dropped into his chair. 'Don't know – Lev seems to think it could have been an accident.'

'His usual bumbling stupidity, you mean,' retorted the lieutenant severely. 'What happened?'

'Smith got on to a train, then hopped off just as it was leaving – appeared to have forgotten his wallet or something – by the time Lev got back, he naturally had vanished.'

'Sounds fishy to me ... couldn't we arrest him on suspicion?'

'We have to convince the Public Prosecutor first ... and he seems to be taking an unusual lack of interest in the case. No, we'll have to sit tight and wait for someone to make a false move.'

Moiseyenko looked impatient. 'But three events now – the attack in Helsinki, the gun in the cabin and the murder …'

Alexei turned up his palms. 'So what – none of those is justification to knock off Smith. The pistol especially – no prints, nothing. We just can't connect it with him.'

Moiseyenko looked dubious. 'You seem to have a soft spot for him – but you must admit, he's the only possible candidate so far.'

'So who attacked him in Finland?– He didn't do that that himself.'

'Could have been some common drunk or thief.'

Pudovkin snorted. 'Now who's talking about coincidences … the obvious answer is that Fragonard was the attacker.'

Vasily nodded slowly. 'That occurred to me, too – and Smith retaliated last night either in revenge or to stop Fragonard having another go at him. But why come right across Europe to act out their vendetta?'

Alexei shook his head ponderously. 'They both came for a reason – but I'm damned if I know what it could be. It's ludicrous to think of espionage agents acting in such a way … perhaps that's why the KGB lads haven't shown up – it's beneath their contempt.'

'Huh – nothing's below that. Those ferrets would spy on a dogfight if they thought one of the animals came from a foreign embassy.'

Alexei found himself scratching his ear. 'I suppose you're right … let's hope the laboratory people turn up something to help us.'

While the two detectives were mulling things over in Petrovka, Simon Smith was coming up the escalator at the

Metro station on Zubovsky Boulevard, just the other side of the Krymsky river bridge from Gorky Park.

As he came out into the sunlight, he hoped that Gustav Pabst would be at the meeting place, after all the trouble he'd had shaking off the militia shadow.

When he had visited the East German's flat the previous evening, he had left that note – written in poor German – to tell the renegade to meet him in Gorky Park with the steel sample, between eleven and twelve that morning.

As Simon's only knowledge of the place was from his city map, he chose the main entrance as the rendezvous point and had asked Pabst to carry two newspapers under his arm as a recognition sign, as neither knew what the other looked like.

Now, as he crossed the bridge over the wide river, he looked to his right and saw the huge expanse of the park stretching down the further bank. Trees and a huge Ferris wheel partly hid the more distant buildings of the Academy of Sciences. In the distance, over the bend in the river, was the green band of the Lenin Hills, with the new skyscraper university needling up to the clouds. His mind was not on scenery, however. He had a sudden nagging fear that perhaps he wasn't so clever after all.

The prospect of walking straight into a trap jumped abruptly into his consciousness and he stopped walking.

For a panic-stricken moment, he almost turned on his heel and walked back to the Metro. Then the cash register in his head jangled to remind him of the two thousand pounds he stood to lose. Anxiety again struggled with avarice, and the greed won. He rapidly changed his plans and instead of walking straight along the pavement to the high, colonnaded entrance a few hundred yards away, he turned sharply down on to the river embankment.

Steps led down from the bridge to a riverside walk, from which many entrances led directly into the park. He sat for a moment on a seat and studied his precious map. In less than two days, it'd had such heavy use that its folds were split, but the part covering the park was good enough to show him the general layout of the main avenues.

Just inside the main gate was a large open space like a parade ground, and from this were many lanes leading to the amusement park, the cafes and the boating lake. He discovered the approximate place where he was sitting and saw if he cut off left, he could approach the inside of the main entrance by a more discreet route.

He stuffed the map back into his raincoat pocket and set off through the rather wild and bushy gardens. Soon the elaborate stonework of the main entrance reared above the next hedge. There were a few people about, mostly old men shuffling about in the sun or playing chess on the park seats, or grandmothers wheeling pushchairs or dragging reluctant children.

He slouched along with his hands in pockets in an effort to look inconspicuous, his eyes rapidly screening the way ahead.

The next corner brought him a view of the large open space inside the gates. It was as big as a football pitch and was covered in loose gravel, not grass. Around the perimeter were benches and banks of shrubs.

He stopped well back from the opening and looked across towards the high entrance. There, tramping up and down the middle of the nearest broad avenue, was a large man in a cheap blue suit, two newspapers firmly rammed under his right armpit.

This must be Gustav Pabst, he thought, with a sudden quickening of his pulse. Again something restrained him from gambolling joyfully across the gravel to pump the German's hand with delight.

He still had this nagging feeling of a baited trap. He was annoyed and told himself that it was the aftermath of being followed by that militiaman … but the sensation persisted. He looked cautiously around the arena at the other actors in the drama.

Three old men walked slowly down the centre of the open space, at an angle to Pabst. A *babushka* pushed a perambulator in the opposite direction and a few women sat gossiping on benches in the middle distance. A park keeper with a large brush and a peaked cap stood idly with his back to Simon, about fifty yards away. The nearest person was a fairly young man, shabbily dressed and hunched up on a bench not twenty yards to his left, again half turned away from the watcher.

Simon watched the tableau tensely for a few moments, keeping well back in the entrance of the smaller path. He was uneasy and afraid to walk out into the big open space.

Pabst, a big red-faced man, reached the end of his pacing in one direction and turned to start tramping back the way he came. Simon was reminded of a bored sentry from his army days – he half expected the man to do a crashing one-two-three about-turn with his big boots at the end of his beat.

Indecisively, he watched. He had chewed his lip so badly that it bled, and still he could not summon up the courage to walk out and challenge Pabst.

For another two minutes, he watched two thousand pounds' worth of humanity crunch up and down the gravel. Pabst turned again and began walking away from him. As he did so, something made Simon glance at the nearest man on the park bench, a slight movement.

It was the first time he had moved. The man brought up his right forefinger and pointed fleetingly at his wristwatch, then at the back of the retreating German. Immediately his hand dropped and he became immobile again, but Simon had seen enough.

With his heart in his mouth, he melted back into the bushes, not waiting to see the 'park keeper' raise the handle of his brush slightly in acknowledgement.

Simon dared not rush, but took a few right angle turns at random until he had put a considerable distance between the parade ground and himself. He snatched another quick look at his map, orientated his position and went out of the park the same way that he had entered.

He hurried back to the underground and caught a central-bound train straight to Sverdlov Square and the Metropol.

Without any pretence at evasion, he galloped up the steps and went to his room, not even noticing that his blue-coated friend was back in position in the foyer.

Simon sank into a chair and made a quick mental inventory of the altered circumstances.

One – I've lost my two thousand quid, he thought, with less distress than he expected – the relief from indecision seemed almost worth it.

Two – Pabst has been rumbled by the Reds and, three – my arrangements for the meeting are also known.

He thought for a moment about how the Fragonard business tied in with this … he couldn't make the two fit together at all. What he was worried about, was the eventual results for himself. The woman in Pabst's apartment block could describe him and identify him if required – and the writing on the note, though unsigned, might be matched with his own, although he *had* used printed capitals.

He was in a fine spot now, he thought desperately – though had he known it, this was the only part of the affair about which he need not have worried.

While he sweated with anxiety upstairs, Lev Pomansky lumbered to the nearest phone to ring Petrovka and a much more unobtrusive watcher slid through the door leading to the cellar under the telephone exchange.

116

Chapter Ten

Later in the morning, a militia car turned out into Petrovka Street and made its way across the centre of Moscow to the Forensic Research Institute. This stood on the Sadovaya Triumfalnaya, part of the tree-lined boulevard that once encircled the old city. Now it was deep in the heart of the capital but still provided a useful link between the radial roads that streamed out from the Kremlin area.

The Volga dropped the detectives outside an old, two-storeyed building that was mature even before the Revolution. It had probably been a merchant's house, though it had no grounds at all, the front door opening directly onto the road.

Alexei had been there before, but it was new to Vasily, who looked up at its faded yellow walls and old-fashioned shutters with undisguised interest.

They walked into an entrance almost pitch-dark after the outside sun. When their eyes adapted, they could see apparatus, refrigerators and all sorts of scientific paraphernalia lining the corridors. There was a strong smell of chemicals, anaesthetics and rabbits, which was unearthly after the dust and sweat of the Petrovka CID.

A door banged open on their left and the big, hearty figure of Gyenka Segel appeared.

'Come – have a look at my treasures!'

They squeezed into a small room having two desks, the owner of the other fortunately being absent.

The pathologist got down to business without delay. 'We haven't had time to do it all yet – the clothing is still being examined – but the tissues from the autopsy are ready.'

He waved towards a small side table where a twin-eyepiece microscope stood with a scatter of glass slides about its base.

'You can look for yourselves if you like, but I think you'd be wasting your time.'

Alexei perched like an old crow on the arm of a chair.

'Just tell us, *tovarishch* ... tell us everything. I want to get my facts straight before I interview these English people at one o'clock.'

Gyenka beamed and handed round cigarettes before launching into his lecture on the mortal remains of Jules Honore Fragonard.

'As I see it, this man had two entirely separate groups of injuries,' he began, 'I suspected this at the autopsy this morning and the microscope confirms it ... and also makes the puzzle all the more difficult to understand.'

Alexei dutifully rose to the bait. He knew that to get the best from Segel, one had to keep playing him like a fish on a hook.

'What's so odd about it, Gyenka Ivanovich?'

The doctor enumerated his points by jabbing a blunt forefinger into the blotter on his desk. 'One ... he had a black eye and a cut on the head, definitely some hours before death. Two ... at the time of death – or very near it – he had blows to his chest and arms. Three ... he was killed by a blow in the neck. Four ... he was dead before he was thrown from that window.' He sat back and smirked with the air of a teacher setting his class a conundrum.

'How can you be certain of this, comrade doctor?' asked Alexei, bravely.

Segel flung an arm in the direction of the microscope.

'There ... we are using a new technique employing enzyme stains ... it came from Finland, quite

118

appropriately, but none the worse for that! It shows that reactions to injury around the eye and head wound were so advanced that at least some hours must have elapsed before death ... for death puts an end to all bodily activities.'

'And the arms and chest?'

'Nothing! This could mean that they were done anything up to an hour or two before death – or even only five minutes, of course.'

'Could the neck blow have been long before death?' asked Vasily, incautiously.

Segel made a face at him. 'My son, if it killed him, it must have been at the time of death, eh?'

Moiseyenko subsided into abashed silence and decided to leave science to the scientists.

Alexei plodded on ... he wanted to get all the information he could before he went back to grill the witnesses at the Metropol.

'And there's no shadow of doubt that he died before he fell from the window.'

Segel pounded his desk with a fist like a ham. 'No, no, no! I tell you, if he had been alive, his heart would have pumped blood from those torn arteries and soaked half a square metre of earth, as well as his horrible pyjamas.'

Pudovkin nodded silently as he orientated the facts in his mind.

'So – someone beats him up twice, kills him and then drops him from the window to try to conceal the murder.' Gyenka Segel nodded. 'A few hours between the beatings – that should help to time the death. I presume no one noticed a black eye before he left the restaurant?'

Moiseyenko came back into the conversation. 'No ... I interrogated the hotel staff – they saw him in the English party up until about eleven o'clock, and there was nothing wrong with his face then.'

The doctor sniffed loudly. 'Eleven o'clock,' he murmured thoughtfully. 'Add at least three hours for these reactions to develop ... that gives the earliest time he could have died as two in the morning – even assuming that he was beaten up immediately he left the dining room.'

Pudovkin shook his head in bewilderment 'Gets worse and worse ... he was probably assaulted late at night, but killed halfway to the dawn ... very odd!'

'Have you got any other information?' asked Segel.

'Damn all! None of the staff heard anything – the old woman on the floor desk swears that no one passed her during the night, so it must be one of the party in that corridor.'

'We know pretty well who it is,' added Moiseyenko darkly.

Segel's face made a big question mark and Alexei told him their background interest in the young man, Simon Smith.

'Seems open-and-shut to me,' commented the pathologist. 'The little Swiss man tries to kill Smith – God knows why – when they were in Finland, so the Englishman retaliates and kills him – intentionally or otherwise.'

Alexei slowly rocked his head back and forth. 'Not so easy as that ... I don't think this Fragonard could have attacked Smith. The differences in size and strength are too great.'

Gyenka snorted. 'Don't you believe it ... I've seen so many things in the last thirty years that I never say nothing can happen now ... a dwarf can throttle an Olympic athlete if the circumstances are right.'

The senior detective looked unconvinced. 'Why all this business of the three hours between the two lots of bruises then?'

Moiseyenko, determined to make his mark, came in again. 'Maybe Smith attacked Fragonard first, then later the Swiss came back to get his revenge and was hit again and killed.'

'In that case, he should have fallen from Smith's window, not his own,' objected Alexei.

'Not if Smith had any sense,' countered Segel. 'With the difference in their physique that you keep talking about, he could easily have taken Fragonard back to his room and tossed him out of the window.'

Alexei still scowled his disbelief. 'I can't see all this happening in the middle of the night without someone hearing something.'

'Only the English were around and they'll stick together and keep their mouths shut,' said Segel.

Alexei got up, grim-faced. 'Then I'll have to find a way to open them – right now,' he growled and led the way to the door.

Slowly and reluctantly, the players in the drama assembled in the fourth floor lounge. It was just on one o'clock and the militia had not yet shown up.

The twittering old ladies, whose names Simon could never recall, were there first. They sat primly and nervously on the edges of two upright chairs – the reverend gentleman came close on their heels and submerged himself apprehensively in an overstuffed velvet armchair.

As Simon and Liz Treasure came down the last stretch of passageway from their rooms, they saw Gilbert Bynge bound with nervous energy up the stairs.

'The Bow Street runners are just coming up in the lift,' he brayed.

A moment later, the grim old woman crashed her gates aside to let out three militiamen. Pudovkin and Moiseyenko had another stolid patrolman with them, who took up the customary position with his back to the lift shaft and stairs. What he was supposed to do, Simon couldn't quite see – none of them had anywhere in which to escape and, so far, no one seemed on the verge of arrest.

The detective captain advanced to the half circle of chairs and settees grouped around the closed television set and nodded a stiff 'Good day' to them.

'Mr Shaw is not here, I see?'

Moiseyenko stepped over to the desk woman and spoke to her. She used her telephone, then shook her head.

'Lying in a drunken stupor somewhere,' said Simon acidly to Liz, then, as if to confound him, a relatively jaunty Michael Shaw appeared. He looked quite respectable for once, his beard combed and his red hair temporarily tidy. He even wore a collar and tie instead of his usual rumpled T-shirt.

'Top of the morning, Oberleutenant!' he said to Pudovkin. 'The diwil if I didn't nearly forget about this little parley.'

Once more he facetiously exaggerated his brogue, but it was lost on Alexei, who gathered the gist of his words, but not the details.

Shaw dropped down on to the settee alongside Elizabeth and pretended to go to sleep.

Pudovkin scowled at him, but began his address to the rest of the group, who were gazing expectantly at him as if waiting to start some innocent party game.

'I regret having to call you together again so soon, but I have grave news that concerns you all – especially one of your number.'

There was a silence so profound that it could almost be reached for and grasped. If Alexei Pudovkin had wanted to start putting the screw on, he could hardly have done better – even the Irishman opened his eyes.

'I have to tell you that your fellow-traveller did not die as the result of an accident – he did not project himself from the window by self-desire.' He paused.

There was only one alternative explanation now, but they all waited like statues to hear the inevitable words fall from his lips.

'Monsieur Fragonard was murdered.'

The detective said this quietly, in slow measured tones, but the effect was profound, especially as he went on, 'I have reason to think … I must think … that the assassin is at present amongst this party.'

There was a silence, then a variety of quiet sounds as the suspects reacted in their various ways.

A few deep sighs, a hysterical twitter from Liz and a muffled curse from Shaw were cut short by Pudovkin.

'Certain examinations have been made and others are to be carried out. I must ask you to co-operate with me and I will do all I can to avoid unpleasantness, which the officials of the Soviet Union wish to do at all times.' He paused and gave each one a piercing look from his dark eyes.

'However, the criminal must be found and will be found. I wish to obtain a sample of each person's fingerprints, please. I have arranged for you all to attend at Militia Headquarters in Petrovka Street at two o'clock. Lieutenant Moiseyenko here will lead you there after lunch. It is a short distance and will take only a few moments.'

He stopped to consult the sheaf of papers in his hands, which Simon recognised as the statements which were taken earlier that day.

Simon rapidly thought about fingerprints and how they might affect him. He had not touched anything in Fragonard's room, except the man's clothing, as far as he remembered, but could he be sure? He leant over to Gilbert who sat alongside the settee. 'They can't take prints without charging somebody, can they? Or with a warrant or something … it's a bloody imposition!'

Gilbert looked uncomfortable. 'I don't know – my prints are bound to be in the jolly room – I'm always in and out of 'em all with bumf and pep talks.'

'Ask him – you're the courier,' urged Simon, clutching at straws.

Pudovkin heard the muttering and looked up sharply.

Gilbert, his tic worse than ever, beat him to the draw and began speaking in Russian. He changed to English after a few words, for the benefit of the others.

'Is this taking of, er … fingerprints … is it legally permissible under the Criminal Code? … we do not have the same compulsion in Britain,' he added, with complete disregard for the truth.

Alexei looked irritated. 'Of course it is legally permissible – I am already doing all I can to spare the innocent among you trouble and embarrassment. The normal procedure would be to conduct you all to Headquarters with a procurator's certificate and detain you there until I was satisfied with the completeness of the evidence.'

'But the fingerprints …?' Gilbert fought doggedly for what he hoped might be their rights.

Pudovkin made short work of him. 'I can also get a procurator's certificate within the hour, if you require this method of progress. If the Procurator's Office takes the case over from the militia – which is very likely in the near future – you will all be subject to more stringent examination.' He wasn't happy with that word 'stringent', but it would have to do.

Alexei turned his eyes down to his papers again. 'I wish to see each person alone, to repeat what is in these statements in the light of our new knowledge.'

Simon wondered icily what the 'new knowledge' was. The half-expected shock of learning that Fragonard had been murdered seemed somehow to be an anti-climax ... his main worry now was that someone else was in on the act, and that Simon Smith, Esq., was again vulnerable.

Pudovkin waved a hand across the lounge. 'I would like each one of you to come into that room when my lieutenant calls you.'

With a frosty smile and a jerky bow of the head, he strode towards an empty bedroom on the corner of the nearest corridor.

Simon watched him go, his wide blue trousers flapping against his legs, revolver bumping on his hip.

Moiseyenko went into the room after him and immediately bounced out again, to summon the nervous vicar to the 'hot seat'.

'Oh, my God, Simon!'

He had almost forgotten Liz's presence beside him, which spoke volumes for his own preoccupation.

'Do you think they'll search our belongings now?' she whispered in a quavering voice. Not 'How awful that he was murdered' or 'I wonder who can have done it', but just this worry about her luggage. He found time to wonder if she was trying to smuggle the Romanov crown jewels out of Russia.

'Search? ... I don't know, I wouldn't be surprised. It would be the sensible thing to do, wouldn't it? As he said, most police forces would be only too eager to turn over every stone in a case like this. From what I've seen of the German *Polizei*, we're having it soft.'

'*So* far, me old lad,' cut in Michael Shaw unexpectedly from the other end of the sofa. 'They're like an iceberg, these lads ... for every bit you see, there's another nine-tenths underground.'

'Personal experience?' asked Simon sweetly, but he really wasn't in the right frame of mind for sarcasm.

He chewed his lip and wondered again what Pudovkin meant by 'new knowledge.' They'd have had a post-mortem, of course – perhaps they were referring to that. He had to decide whether to stick to his story or not … he had to explain away his dodging the chap in the Metro, too. If he couldn't convince them that that was an accident, he was in it up to the armpits.

The vicar came out very quickly, looking so relieved that he almost danced across to the two old ladies to reassure them, but Moiseyenko politely steered him away and called one of them – a Miss Carruthers – into Pudovkin's room. She stayed in for an even shorter period than the vicar; so did her friend, the other aged lady.

Then it was the turn of Elizabeth Treasure. She went as pale as a corpse as Vasily called her name. Simon gave her hand a last squeeze and made a discreet 'sssh' with his lips. She smiled weakly and nodded down at him. As he watched her wonderful body undulating across the lounge, he gave a quiet sigh of relief that she seemed intent on shielding him over the matter of his visit to Fragonard's room last night.

She was in the room appreciably longer than the others. Though the time seemed an eternity to Simon, his watch said that it was only four minutes before the door opened and Moiseyenko ushered her out.

Ideologies apart, it was obvious that the young bachelor lieutenant was quite impressed with her sophisticated charms.

She made as if to come over to Simon, but Moiseyenko touched her arm and pointed in the direction of her room. He said something to her and, with a little shrug of apology in Simon's direction, she vanished.

Gilbert went next, his mouth twitching in top gear. Simon timed him at only two minutes. He came out wiping his brow with a handkerchief and set off down the stairs in search of a stiff drink.

'Like the "ten little nigger boys" – only there's seven of us!' observed Shaw heartily. He had been slumped in the corner of the big settee, but now he unwound his great hairy body and planted his hands on his knees in expectation. 'Who's it going to be next – you or me?'

'I'm always last when they're giving things away,' said Simon, in a poor attempt at nonchalance.

'They're obviously taking us in reverse order of suspicion, me lad! So we'll soon know who's number one of their "Top of the Chops".'

His facetiousness jarred horribly on Simon's nerves. Shaw's whole manner seemed out of character at the moment … normally inert, apathetic, sometimes sullen, he was now taking a whimsical interest in what was going on – *very odd*, thought Simon.

Moiseyenko came out of the bedroom door again like a cuckoo from a clock. 'Mr Shaw!' he called across the lounge, deserted now except for the two men, the waiting militia sentry and the old woman.

Michael got up lazily.

'Hard luck, old feller … looks as if you're the one.' He drew a finger across his throat and made a revolting slashing sound. He sauntered across and disappeared into the bedroom.

As slowly as time had gone before, now it shot past as soon as the door closed behind Shaw. Though he did not have the heart to time it, it seemed only seconds before the bearded writer was out again and Moiseyenko was beckoning him across the carpet.

With a conscience feeling like a half a ton of lead in his stomach, he went into the spare bedroom and stood nervously facing Pudovkin. The detective sat behind the writing desk and waved a bony hand at a hard chair set opposite him.

Simon lowered himself gingerly, while Moiseyenko went around to stand at his captain's shoulder.

The prime suspect had a sudden mental flashback to twenty years before, when he had sat timidly before his headmaster and form master for some minor crime at his grammar school. Now the stakes were much higher – perhaps his liberty for a long time.

'Mr Simon Smith,' stated Alexei, pondering over the inevitable papers. His head was bent down and Simon stared at his stubbly grey hair, sticking up over the crown like some moulting rooster. He lifted his head and looked the Englishman hard in the eyes. His face was stern, but no arrogance or cruelty showed itself.

'I must tell you at the start that the criminal is one of your party – and of those, you are by far the most obvious suspect.'

The prime suspect felt no particular emotion at this, only a heightening of his wariness. He wondered with almost detached interest why the militia were giving him the shortest odds.

'Have you anything you wish to tell me at this stage?' asked Pudovkin severely. *Obviously fishing for a confession*, thought Simon, shaking his head silently.

'You are very sure of that?'

Alexei stared at Simon's face as if waiting for some sign of guilt to appear, but the Englishman managed to keep up his expression of injured innocence.

Pudovkin proceeded to fill him in with a few proofs of his villainy.

'Before this tragedy occurred, you were already under surveillance – so it is only logical that we should be highly suspicious of you and your motives – a suspicion that has been strengthened by your recent actions.'

This roundabout speech seemed to have been a strain on Pudovkin's English and helped to break the tension that in any other circumstances would have been a useful tool in any interrogator's armoury.

Simon kept his impassive face, but it also was a strain. This was the first he knew of any surveillance *before* Fragonard's death – why the hell was that? Had 'Tool Steel' been sprung to the Soviets in some way? Were they just playing him along before arresting him?

Pudovkin unconsciously put his mind at rest on that score, but threw yet another bombshell at him with his next speech.

'When you returned to the *Yuri Dolgorukiy* in Helsinki after your unfortunate "accident", the ship's doctor saw bruises on your neck which were undoubtedly the result of attempted strangulation. You did not report this, but lied about the nature of the injury. No criminal elements are welcome in the Soviet Union from outside, but as it seemed that you were the victim, rather than the perpetrator, we decided not to bar you.'

He stopped again and searched the Englishman's face for signs of remorse. Simon smiled back weakly and ran a nervous hand over his hair.

Pudovkin sighed quietly and went back to the attack.

'Before the vessel could get to Leningrad, this was found in your cabin!'

He dipped in his battered briefcase as he spoke and tossed the automatic pistol across the desk. It fell with a clatter in front of Simon and lay menacingly on the dark wood, a luggage label still tied to the trigger guard.

If Alexei had been trying for some response, he got it this time. Simon went red in the face, his feelings genuinely outraged this time. 'This is bloody ridiculous! I've never had a gun in my life, except in the Army. They didn't find this in my cabin, I can assure you!'

'And I assure you they did – hidden beneath the mattress.'

Simon reached out and snatched up the pistol. Moiseyenko jerked into readiness, though he realized a second later that it was unloaded. Simon merely turned it

129

over in his hand and slid it almost contemptuously back across the desk.

'If it *was* found there, then someone planted it on me.'

His anger had temporarily driven out his uneasiness, but Alexei was still master of the interview.

'Even if you tell the truth about this gun, the weapon was still placed there to incriminate you ... so why? And why should someone want to kill you?'

This brought Simon up short. His outrage evaporated and he had to think fast. 'I don't know ... someone did jump on me in Helsinki – I didn't see them. It must have been a common thief, that's all.'

Pudovkin slid the next question in smoothly.

'A common thief ... and what did they steal from you?'

Simon's brain seized up. *He's got me cold*, he thought desperately. *If I say 'my wallet', they can easily find that I still have it.*

'And why did you not tell all this to the ship's officers, instead of some childish story about falling in the dock ... you had nothing to hide, so you say?'

The militia officer shook his head dolefully. 'No, Mr Smith, you were "up to something" ... I think that is the expression. Within a day of this, one of your fellow travellers is found murdered. This is too much a coincidence!'

He stopped and stared at Simon expectantly, waiting for some answer. Simon thought desperately and then muttered some banal excuse about not wanting to be delayed in Helsinki by raising a fuss with the police, but he found that the other was not listening ... Moiseyenko was whispering into his senior's ear.

Pudovkin nodded impatiently and waved the lieutenant away. 'Now, we come to this morning. You deliberately tricked one of my officers who was quite justifiably watching you ... on the Metro, you eluded him. Why was this?'

Simon had been waiting for this one and had his injured innocence expression ready for use 'I'd no idea anyone was following me ... I don't know how I could have eluded him, if I didn't know he was there.'

Pudovkin patiently explained the rout of Lev Pomansky at the Mayakovskaya station.

'Oh, that ... I thought I had forgotten my wallet and jumped off the train to make sure,' he said airily.

'The wallet that *wasn't* stolen from you by the thief in Finland?' asked Alexei sarcastically.

He passed on to the next episode.

'Now we must speak of last evening. You say in your statement that ...'

They went over it all again, every movement from the time the party broke up until the next morning. At the end of every sentence, Pudovkin rubbed in the fact that Simon was Suspect Number One and did he now want to tell the truth and make a confession.

The treatment was most effective and at the end of fifteen minutes, Simon was sweating and ready to start shouting the truth just to shut the other man up. Then, for some reason, the detective stopped just in time and Simon's self-control held out, with little to spare.

Another couple of minutes would have had him pouring out his story of his visit to Fragonard's room, though even then he would have hung fire on the basic facts of the tool steel.

This deep urgent desire for self-purgation came as a shock to Simon, when later that day he went over the interview in his mind. The old police trick of endless repetition of the questions by a relay of questioners, used by every police force in the world, was a most effective means of breaking down resistance ... Moiseyenko had joined in with Pudovkin in turn. Abruptly, Pudovkin stopped and stood up, his fists leaning heavily on the desk.

'You may go for the present. I am afraid that we may need to see you before long.'

There seemed no more to be said and Simon thankfully hurried from the room. He felt later that he should have put up some sort of bluster, on the principle that attack is the best form of defence. But a shouting match with Pudovkin seemed futile – no amount of yelling to see the British Consul would have cut any ice with him. When it came to the point, Simon was glad enough to scurry out with his tail between his legs, thankful that he had not done himself irretrievable damage by some rash answers.

He went towards his room, intending to wash the perspiration from his brow before collecting Liz Treasure for lunch.

As he passed a small side corridor near his room, Michael Shaw turned out of it. It was too well-timed to be a coincidence.

'How did it go?' asked the Irishman.

Simon rolled his eyes at the ceiling 'Bloody awful – they must be round the twist. The senior bobby accused me point-blank of doing in old Fragonard.'

Shaw grinned at him crookedly. 'Well, *didn't* you?'

He leaned against the wall and regarded the suspect with open amusement.

Simon's temper, rubbed raw by recent events, flared up at once.

'What's so damn funny? I'm in a spot – a conspiracy, organised by that little bastard that's dead!'

Shaw heaved himself off the wall and grabbed Simon's arm.

'Come up to my room – we've got some talking to do.'

Simon, feeling that he'd heard those words before in this very corridor, was half dragged along to Room 516, three doors up from his own and next door to the murder room.

Shaw slammed the door behind them, tore off his jacket and dragged the tie from his throat with a grunt of relief. Looking more his usual untidy self, he went into the bathroom and came out with a bottle of Dimple Haig and two glasses. Without a word, he splashed two liberal measures into each and thrust one into Simon's hand.

'Now, let's get down to business.'

He swallowed half his drink, put the glass on the bedside table and hurled himself full-length onto the eiderdown.

Simon still stood in the centre of the room, looked sulky and bewildered, as Shaw hoisted his back up against the top of the bed and folded his arms behind his neck.

'Sorry about the throat, lad, but those who play with fire are likely to get hurt.'

This was too much for Simon. He put the untasted whisky down and grabbed the rail at the bottom of the bed. 'Now what the hell do you mean by that?' he demanded shakily.

Shaw waved his hand impatiently 'Aw, the saints preserve us! Can't you see the nose on your own face?' His more genuine Irish accent broke through instead of his artificial brogue. 'As that fool Fragonard told you last night, I can't understand why an old hand like Harry Kramer picked a raw amateur for a job as important as this.'

A star shell seemed to go off inside Simon's head. *God, here's another of them*, he thought desperately.

Shaw swigged the rest of his drink and stared at the younger man. His good humour had evaporated and he looked callous and impatient.

'To save your endless, foolish questions, get this straight once and for all ... 'twas I that tried to do away with you in Helsinki; I planted that ruddy pistol on you. *And* I killed Fragonard last night – or this morning, to be more accurate.'

133

He suddenly uncoiled from the bed and stood towering over Simon.

'And get this! I'm collecting that steel sample from Gustav Pabst ... so if you want to keep on breathing, keep out of my way.'

Simon had been silent through all this – not because there was anything wrong with his voice, but because his mind was so overwhelmed that it had no time to spare for his vocal cords. At last, he got his brain into commission again and came up with a choice selection of swear words, which he flung at Shaw with the uttermost venom that he could muster.

The bearded 'journalist' appeared to take no offence. 'All right, all right, spare us the cussing, lad,' he sighed, when Simon ran out of breath and inspiration 'Just get this clear ... I heard you in the room next door last night. Heard every word, in fact, as I had me ear to the door panels there. Dam' nearly got deafened when you smacked the old man up against the doorpost, incidentally. Now, if you don't keep your nose out of my business, I'll have a sudden return of my memory and tell Comrade Pudovkin that I heard the sound of your voice and a scuffle and few other details, like you tiptoeing away down the corridor afterwards ... got a darling imagination, have I! You're already in big trouble with the rozzers and that would just about nail you for good.'

Simon jumped at him and grabbed him by the shirt front, but he was not dealing with Fragonard now. With a contemptuous twitch, Shaw flung him off like a mastiff getting rid of a toy poodle. Simon staggered back and fell against the wardrobe, hitting his shoulder painfully.

'Don't be silly, chum ... I can't afford to bounce another out of the window just now – two in a day is a bit much.' Shaw calmly picked up Simon's whisky and drained it at a gulp.

'Tell me how far you've got with this Pabst character. Fragonard spilt all the beans to me that he had from Kramer ... a few little raps with me knuckles on his pressure points made him sing like a canary, but he didn't seem to have got the actual rendezvous points out of you. So save me the trouble, will you – and talk.'

Simon nursed his shoulder. 'You can't get away with this!' He sounded like the hero of a corny novelette, he realized, but it was happening, so he had to accept it. 'You killed Fragonard ... I'll tell the militia, they'll soon check on your movements.'

He was mouthing nonsense and he dribbled to a halt. He dare not say anything to the militia – he was already in a spot; any more voluntary statements and he would be in it right up to his injured neck.

Shaw watched his mind working and grinned sardonically. 'No, you can't, can you – so now, spill it, there's a good boy.'

Simon backed away and said, 'To hell with you!'

Shaw hardly moved his body, but his long arm shot out and a bundle of knuckles hit Simon just above the elbow, where the radial nerve lies just under the surface. He grunted with an excruciating pain and turned white, as his fingers went dead.

Shaw pushed him down into a nearby chair.

'Now cut it out, sonny, or I'll make you feel as if you'd spent a day inside a cement mixer! Tell me about Pabst, or I'll squeak to the coppers.'

Simon felt sick with pain – he could understand now why Fragonard talked just before Shaw killed him. He managed to speak through clenched teeth.

'Why should they believe you? It's your word against mine.'

'You're in the mire already, Jack – they'll believe anything against you if it helps hook you. And your girlfriend won't last long when old Hawk-eye Pudovkin gets cracking on her.'

Simon looked wildly at Shaw. 'Leave her out of this.'

'Be damned will I! She was in your room last night – I was peeping, I'm afraid. Not really so drunk as I try to make out, you know … it's a good act that, more pleasant than false noses and stick-on moustaches.'

He grinned and poured himself another whisky – none for Simon this time.

'Aye, you lucky old satyr – she was in there, and I'm quite ready to say that I heard her voice in the corridor.'

'You bastard! How do you spend your holidays … looking through bedroom keyholes.'

Shaw laughed, then punched him again on the same arm, though not so hard this time. 'I've been keeping tabs on Fragonard since London. I knew he'd got to Kramer and had the dope on this steel stuff from him. I nearly lost him after that but found he'd joined this ship, in Copenhagen. I had to fly all the way to Stockholm to get a free berth. It wasn't until the night of that party that I tumbled that you were the chap he was following.'

'So you tried to get me out of the way in Finland,' said Simon bitterly.

'I slipped up there – you must tell me how you managed it sometime. I'll meet you in London if you don't land in some Russian nick … we'll have a few pints and a chat.'

'Go to hell.'

Simon was beginning to think that he had stepped into someone's nightmare – he had met two self-confessed murderers in the space of just over twelve hours and now one of them was proposing cosy meetings with one of the intended victims.

'If you were so clever in getting Fragonard to talk, why bother with me – you're so keen on telling me what small fry I am.'

Shaw punched his own hand, almost gaily. 'Ha! I'm getting old or somet'in … slipped up again last night. I got half the yarn from him, when the old devil turned nasty on me and tried to pull a knife when I wasn't looking. He tried to puncture me gizzard and I had to let him have a quick one across the throat, just to quieten him, but the old goat dropped dead on me, blast him. Good job he didn't have a gun.'

'He did – but I dropped it in his lavatory cistern.'

Shaw gave a great bellow of laughter, genuine and unrestrained.

'Be damned you did! … *now* I can tell the militia that I heard you clanking around with the bog – they'll look inside and – wow! Your suspect rating will go up off the scale!'

Simon cursed his big mouth. His brain worked overtime while Shaw chattered on – the glimmerings of an idea flickered in his agile mind.

Shaw was still talking. '… so with the little feller dead, I'd lost me chance of getting these details of the contact with Pabst. I've got his address, but I'm sure that you've fixed up something already to collect the stuff from him.' He jabbed a great finger almost in Simon's eye. 'So talk, or I'll be after having a few words with the constabulary about you!'

Simon rapidly made up his mind and took the plunge.

'All right, you great slob … but if anything goes wrong, boy, I'll drag you right in after me.' He took a deep breath. 'I've arranged to meet Pabst tomorrow morning in Gorky Park, just inside the main entrance. He's to carry two folded newspapers under his right arm … he should have the steel with him, so it will be easy, blast you!'

Privately, he prayed that the same reception party would be there as this morning, all ready to jump on Shaw as soon as he showed the slightest interest in the man in the blue suit.

137

Chapter Eleven

The taking of the fingerprints proved less terrifying than the band of suspects had expected.

Moiseyenko sent a wooden-faced militiaman to escort them to Petrovka. He spoke indifferent English, but managed to lead them out into Sverdlov Square. Like an anxious sheepdog with a reluctant flock, he herded them up Petrovka Street and ushered them into a room on the ground floor of Militia Headquarters.

It was barely furnished with a table and a few hard chairs. Simon, feeling strangely placid now that his mission had failed so utterly, tried to distract the very uneasy Elizabeth by pointing out the only decoration – a faded red banner on the wall, which bore the curious exhortation "Plant more trees in ravines and gullies". Their debate over this agricultural motto in the heart of Moscow was interrupted by the arrival of two technicians with the paraphernalia of fingerprinting. With deft efficiency, they set up their rollers and pads and within five minutes had taken two full-handed 'dabs' from all seven of the British party.

Almost before they knew it, they were all out on the sidewalk again, blinking in the afternoon sun, free again for at least the rest of the afternoon.

The rest of the Trans-Europa tour, the innocents from the third floor, were already at the Tretyakov Art Gallery with an Intourist guide, and Gilbert Bynge hurried after them, taking the vicar and two old ladies. Simon and Liz opted out and Michael Shaw, who had not said another word to Simon since the lunchtime meeting, vanished alone in a taxi.

'Don't fancy an art gallery, somehow,' said Simon, as he stood with Liz outside the militia entrance.

'Too right – I never go near these cultural places in London, so why should I feel obliged to see them here?' replied the girl, with an irreverence that would have shocked the culture-loving natives.

'Let's go down and have another look at Red Square and the Kremlin ... take our minds off things,' he suggested.

In fact, the first place that they visited when they got to the huge square was not an historic monument, but the GUM Stores, the largest departmental shop in Russia. Its ornate bulk spread down the better part of the Square opposite Lenin's Tomb and even though Simon's declared hatred of shops made him reluctant, he admitted that the experience was worthwhile.

They carefully kept their conversation off the subject of murder, militia and interrogation, talking with forced interest about the immediate sights and sounds.

The GUM was a series of glass-roofed arcades, side by side, which stretched for hundreds of yards in both directions away from the main entrance. A large fountain played in the centre of the store, squirting its jets up to the first floor balcony.

'More like a market than a shop,' said Liz, fascinated in spite of her worries. They walked around the galleries, looking at the hundreds of individual shops that lined them. Upstairs, they paused to lean over the balcony and look down at the crowded ground floor. A great throng of Muscovites, round-capped Armenians, Mongols from further east, and even some gypsies, jostled between the rows of open-fronted shops.

'Looks like a cross between Petticoat Lane and King's Cross station,' observed Elizabeth.

'Yes, plenty of stuff here – everything from mink coats to outboard motors, but some of it's a helluva price!'

The mention of money seemed to subdue Liz, but Simon was not in a sensitive enough mood to notice.

They left the GUM, walked across the square and entered the Kremlin through the Spasskaya gate. For an hour they wandered around the gardens and gold-capped churches, again being partly successful in losing their preoccupation in a wonderland of tourism. They duly saw the picture-postcard attractions – the Tsar Cannon and the cracked bell and spent an envious half-hour staring at the treasures in the Kremlin Museum.

Then Elizabeth declared teatime and they began walking slowly back to the Metropol.

Several times she looked back over her shoulder and became more and more agitated.

'I'm sure someone is following us,' she hissed at Simon as they passed the red brick of the Lenin Museum. 'Look behind,' she ordered.

Sure enough, fifty yards to their rear was the now familiar figure of Lev Pomansky, plodding along in their wake.

'That's all right – he's trailing me, not you. Been after me all day ... I got a row from the coppers, in fact, for accidentally throwing him off the scent on the underground this morning.'

He managed to convey an air of blasé nonchalance about this, as if being followed by Soviet militiamen was an everyday thing in his life.

She looked around again, only partly reassured. 'Hope you're right. I don't want one after me, thank you.'

Before going to the smaller café just inside the main entrance of the Metropol, they made the long trip to their rooms to freshen up. Simon tapped on her door when he was ready and went in to find her touching up her war paint in front of a mirror.

141

As he waited, she abruptly asked, 'Any idea where the street markets would be in Moscow?'

He shook his head into the mirror as he stood behind her and put his hands around her waist. 'Not the faintest – why do you ask?'

She shrugged. 'Just wondered. I heard they were interesting; the only places where private enterprise is still allowed. Farm people selling their stuff and all that.'

This seemed altogether out of character for the sophisticated Elizabeth. *Her only interest in markets is likely to be those in Kensington High Street*, he thought cynically.

As she repainted her eyes, he looked around the room, thinking that it was yet another replica of Fragonard's, Shaw's and his own … he seemed to have been in nearly all the rooms now. His eye caught the intriguing brown case, this time perched perilously on top of the chest of drawers. The key was in the lock and he had a sudden silly urge to go over and open it.

At that moment, Liz looked down and said a rude word. 'My stockings – a hole in the ankle, that's *your* damned Kremlin gardens!'

She went over to the brown case and opened it.

Simon followed her and looked over her shoulder, half expecting to see it stuffed with contraband American cigarettes or hashish. All he saw was a rather untidy assortment of underclothes and packets of nylons.

Elizabeth, unaware of how close he was, suddenly stepped back with a pair of stockings and tripped over his foot.

With a squeal of dismay, she staggered and grabbed at the case for support. It crashed down from the chest and a corner caught on one of the brass handles of the lower drawer.

There was a ripe tearing sound as brown Rexine ripped apart.

142

With a look of utter stupefaction, Simon watched a blue shower of crisp five-pound notes erupt across the bed from the false bottom of the case.

After eighty five-pound notes fluttered to the carpet from the ripped case, Liz stood aghast for a second then threw herself on them and scrabbled them together.

'You silly great idiot – I thought you would have had more sense than to try a mad caper like this!'

Anger at Elizabeth's folly made his usually deferential manner to her drop away like a discarded mask. He sat on the edge of her bed and glared at her with a mixture of exasperation and concern.

Liz Treasure lay across the top of the eiderdown, tearful but obstinate.

'I need the money, Simon – my God, you'll never know how much we need it! The business is on the rocks, yet with that little bit more capital, it would be a goldmine … my friend said …'

'To the devil with your damned friend! She needs her own mind spring-cleaned for dreaming up such a crazy scheme as this. Let her come and do her own dirty work!'

He jumped up and stalked the room in agitation. 'Don't you realize that you could get twenty years in a labour camp for this sort of thing! In Russia, "speculating" in a foreign currency is about the worst crime in the book … murder is peanuts compared to it. They actually shot four blokes for it last year!'

She snivelled into her handkerchief. 'It would have been all right if all this fuss about that awful little man hadn't cropped up.'

'Like hell it would! … my God, I've got troubles enough of my own over that, but I can still go cold all over when I think of you trying to peddle four hundred quid in fivers around the streets of Moscow, looking for a black market money changer.'

'The idea was good,' she mumbled through her sniffs.

'"*Was*" is the right word!' he snapped, 'That racket fizzled out over a year ago. The days when Western tourists sold everything except their underpants for roubles have gone – and so has this currency racket.'

They sat in stony silence for a moment, the woman sulking and Simon going over this latest crisis in his mind.

Explanations were obviously called for. Bit by bit, the whole story came out. Elizabeth's presence on the Trans-Europa trip was no holiday. With her boutique in the financial doldrums, she had raised enough for the fare and borrowed another two hundred pounds. Together with another two hundred put up by her partner-friend, she had set sail for Russia with the intention of quadrupling their investment, at the very least.

The friend had known someone who had worked a similar racket on a smaller scale a couple of years before, discovering that although the official exchange rate was just over two roubles to the pound, Western currency was so much sought after that twenty, thirty and sometimes even forty roubles could be got on the black market.

The contacts for this profitable game were to be found, allegedly, in the furtive men who hung about restaurants and street markets, on the lookout for Western tourists.

'But what on earth are the use of these roubles?' Simon had objected. 'Even if you get them back to London, who wants Russian paper money?'

'One doesn't take roubles!' was Liz's explanation. 'There are several State-owned antique and jewellery stores both here and in Leningrad, where stuff from before the Revolution is sold, mainly to West European and American tourists. With these extra roubles, one can buy some really valuable small stones that would more than hold their price when one sold them again in London.'

'But the shops would surely be suspicious of someone flashing hundreds of quid's worth of roubles about!'

'You have to be sensible about it,' came the persuasive reply. 'Not to buy too much in the same shop and to spread the purchases between several people.' She had looked spaniel-eyed at Simon. 'Actually, I was going to ask you to help me a bit there. Of course, one would have to smuggle them back into England, or the duty will kill any profit, but with rings or loose stones, that would be child's play.'

'So *you* say ... I think you're round the bloody twist to think you could get away with it, in the best of circumstances ... and now, of course, you've really had it – thank God I found out before you got yourself into real trouble.'

He talked to her like a rather irate Dutch uncle and convinced her that not only was her information out of date, due to the Soviet authorities getting wise to the racket, but that since the murder, they were all under surveillance. 'You saw that chap today in Red Square – he was after me, but I'll bet if you wandered out looking for some black marketeers, they'd be on you like a ton of bricks.'

He turned to her now, as she lay dabbing her nose delicately with her handkerchief.

'And you can forget any idea of trying to take that English money back with you – you can't repair that amateur false bottom on your case and we're sure to get our belongings searched at any moment, now that Pudovkin's really on the warpath over Fragonard. You'll have to get rid of it – straight away. Flush it down the loo, if you take my tip.'

This just about sent her berserk. Money seemed the substitute for babes-in-arms to Liz Treasure, when it came to protective instinct. She sobbed and argued and wailed – even pounded his chest in temper – but he remained adamant.

Suddenly she capitulated. 'All right, damn you, but it will finish the shop. It's not even my money – half was borrowed, the other half is my friend's … as well as the hundred extra for this trip.'

'It's that or the prospect of a Russian prison for a few years … and if you got past them, the British authorities would hammer you for illegally taking currency out of the country – so make your choice, but make it quickly.'

He offered to do the flushing act for her there and then, to get it over with as painlessly as possible, but here she was immovably obstinate.

'I'll get drunk tonight and do it myself,' she said sullenly. '… what a hell of a trip; all we want now is for the ship to sink on the way home and that would be the hat-trick!'

Simon kissed her unresponsive mouth and went back to his room to ponder his own troubles.

Chapter Twelve

The telephone in Alexei Pudovkin's box-like office rang on the average about once every six minutes – he had once taken the trouble to work this out over a period of a few days.

In the late afternoon of the day of the murder, it rang with its usual insistence and he heard the fruity voice of Gyenka Segel at the other end.

He listened to the voluble doctor and replied in monosyllables. Then he slipped a hand over the mouthpiece and yelled for Moiseyenko, who appeared instantly as if summoned by Aladdin.

Still listening and muttering an occasional agreement, Pudovkin rapidly scribbled a note on a pad and pushed it across to Vasily. The lieutenant read it, registered delight and galloped out of the office. He ran all the way downstairs and only rank prevented him from running to the Metropol. He walked there as fast as he could, consistent with the dignity of a militia officer.

At the hotel, he went straight up to the fourth floor and went to the guardian virgin at the desk. She shook her head at his quick question and handed him a key. He hurried around the passageways and stopped at Room 513. As he reached the prime suspect's door, he was glad that Smith was not in – it would save a lot of talking and perhaps foolish objections that the man might have to having his property examined.

Moiseyenko was convinced that Simon was the killer and could hardly understand why the Procurator's Office had not already issued a warrant for his arrest.

He opened the door and looked quickly around to make sure that no clothing was lying around. Then he strode to the large wardrobe and pulled it open to see a row of shirts, some pullovers and two suits hanging there. Checking against the scrap of paper that Pudovkin had thrust at him, he ignored everything except the suits. With a grunt of satisfaction, he took down a hanger carrying a mid-grey tweed and folded it unceremoniously over his arm.

Leaving the room without another glance, he hurried back to Petrovka and picked up a vehicle in the transport pool to take his latest trophy down to the Forensic Institute.

'More brandy, Vasily Sergeyevich – we needn't go back to Headquarters for another hour yet.'

Alexei Pudovkin, relaxed in braces and shirtsleeves, pushed the bottle across the table, while Darya stalked out of the room, disapproval oozing from every pore.

Alexei would not have bothered to have come home at all this evening, but, for the sake of peace, he thought that he had better make some pretence at cohabitation with his wife.

He brought Moiseyenko up to supper with him. Darya, who disapproved of the young man as much as she did any of Pudovkin's militia friends below the rank of major, grudgingly made them a meal before they went back to Petrovka to see the commissioner.

The affair at the Metropol had brought back a lot of life into Alexei. Vasily could see the change in twenty-four hours; the older man was more alert, more alive and even the lines around his mouth seemed less dejected than yesterday.

He had even faced up to Darya over the business of the laundry and told her bluntly that work came first and if she wanted the stuff taken, she could go herself. To cap this, he had even switched off the television in the middle of her favourite programme, when Vasily arrived. She seemed to accept this show of daring independence without much fight – a sulky acceptance seemed to be the order of the day. Alexei began to wonder if there was any truth in the old saying that women like to be dominated – she had even capitulated over the choice of their summer holiday – his Baltic fishing had triumphed over her eternal Crimea.

The meal over, the two militiamen sat at the table with coffee and a bottle of spirits, talking over the latest developments in the 'affair Fragonard'.

'I wonder how long Segel will be,' pondered Moiseyenko. He had delivered the suit to the house on Sadovaya Triumfalnaya and the doctor had promised to ring as soon as they got a definite answer, his technicians working on after hours until the job was done.

'We'll wait for him to ring before going to see Father Mitin,' said Alexei, pouring another drink. 'As long as it's not later than nine o'clock – the old man likes to go to meet his pals in the Armenia on a Friday night.'

Moiseyenko looked at Darya's elaborate electric clock on the wall.

'Another hour … I can't understand why the Prosecutor is hanging fire over this one.'

Pudovkin shrugged. 'I'll ask the Colonel tonight – I've a feeling that there must have been a whisper from over the Kremlin wall about it. But if *tovarishch* Segel turns up with his proof tonight, we'll have no option but to collect Smith and dump him in the Procurator's lap.'

Vasily nodded and Alexei, with an abandon which surprised even himself, yelled to Darya to bring the coffee pot. She appeared in the doorway, looked at her husband with a curious expression that he could not analyse and placed the pot in the centre of the table. Back in the kitchen, the usual thunderous clashing of crockery was strangely muted.

Moiseyenko winked at the older man and grinned. 'What have you done to her – given her a good walloping?'

Alexei grunted. 'It's too good to last – she'll probably creep up on me in the night and stab me in the back.'

The phone shrilled suddenly. He could never get away from it, but this time, the call was welcome.

'Pudovkin … good evening, Gyenka Ivanovich … yes.' There was a long, pregnant silence, then, 'Yes, yes thank you … goodnight.'

With slow deliberation, Pudovkin dropped the receiver and came back to the table. His lieutenant was almost pop-eyed with anticipation.

'Well?' he asked.

Alexei picked up his uniform jacket and hung it around his bony shoulders. 'Let's go back to Petrovka,' he said gravely.

Colonel Igor Mitin restlessly paced his room, glaring at the clock every minute, thinking of his cronies getting a head start on him in the restaurant of the Armenia hotel on Neglinnaya Street. Then there was a rap on the door and Pudovkin loped in. He threw a perfunctory salute in the direction of his chief.

'Took your time, Alexei Alexandrovich,' grumbled Mitin. 'Sit down and let's have a nice quick version of what's been going on – nobody tells me anything; of course. I'm always the last to know.'

Pudovkin crouched on a small chair opposite the obese colonel and gave a succinct account of the day's activities. He knew quite well that Mitin had been getting reports on everything except the latest development, but it was part of the fat man's act to pretend to be neglected by his staff.

150

The news about Simon Smith's suit made him sit up and drop the façade of the forgotten chief. He quietly took out a packet of cigarettes and slid one over to Alexei, who explained the findings at the Forensic Institute.

'Segel said that they found some tiny grey, black and white fibres on the front of Fragonard's woollen dressing gown, over the chest and waist area. They were totally different in colour and texture to any of the dead man's clothing, so we took a chance on looking at Smith's suits. The waiters in the Metropol restaurant remembered vaguely that he had a grey suit on last evening, so Moiseyenko collected the only grey suit in his wardrobe and we took it to Gyenka Segel.'

He paused to light his cardboard cigarette.

'Segel's men now say that the fibres are identical – the ones from the suit exactly match the ones from Fragonard's body – some were wool and the rest were a synthetic fibre the English call Terylene. The colour, thickness and chemical properties were identical and the cloth is totally different from anything we make in the Soviet Union – naturally, we've got plenty of synthetic fibres, but they're not the same as this stuff.'

Mitin bobbed his head over his four chins – he had even forgotten the clock for the moment. 'So the front of Smith's suit was pressed against Fragonard's dressing gown,' he summarised.

'Yes – either when he struggled with him or when he lifted the body to throw it from the window.'

'Or both,' added Mitin unnecessarily.

Pudovkin scratched his chin 'I suppose so – yet it seems extraordinary – a man comes a couple of thousand miles from his home to kill another total stranger in circumstances where he's bound to be caught. No one could say that we've overtaxed our brains today – the forensic people have done all the work.'

151

Mitin heaved his great shoulders and scratched his ear. 'That's not our worry, Alexei Alexandrovich … we've got to take him now.'

Alexei nodded 'I can't see anything to stop us arresting him now – we'd be wrong not to, I suppose. Trouble and violence seem to follow him around.'

'The sooner the better,' agreed the colonel, picking up his phone.

'I'll get on to the Prosecutor's Office and tell whoever is on call. They won't do anything until the morning, but at least they can't say that we didn't tell them as soon as we knew.'

While he waited for the official to be traced, Alexei sounded Mitin out about the background.

'There's something odd about this case – we've no idea about a motive and I feel sure that the boys from The Centre are not far behind us.'

The Commissioner sniggered. 'Behind us! … they may well be way out ahead.'

Pudovkin's eyebrows went up. 'Have you heard anything, then?'

The colonel did his jowl-shaking routine again. 'No, not a sound from that direction, but I know that the Prosecutor had word from the Ministry of the Interior yesterday that he was not to take any action on that pistol from the ship until further notice.'

'What's that mean – do we have to stay clear as well?'

Igor Mitin was so engrossed with the problem that he actually put his forefingers in each of his ears and wiggled them around, to Alexei's profound revulsion. Then he picked up the phone again as he was connected with the Prosecutor's Office.

When the call was finished, he returned to the same topic.

'I guess that the KGB were waiting to jump on somebody over that gun and didn't want us blundering into their ambush. I might be wrong,' he added virtuously.

Alexei was more interested in immediate action. 'So can we go ahead? This man Smith needs picking up tonight, though my old police nose tells me that something smells here.'

Mitin drew careful circles on his blotter. 'Carry on, Alexei ... the Ministry told the Prosecutor, not us – we're not supposed to know. I only got it on the grapevine. And that was only about the ship affair – there hadn't been a murder then. Let the cloak-and-dagger men sort it out later.'

Pudovkin muttered agreement, and Mitin began to look anxiously at the clock again. 'I've got an important meeting in a few minutes, so if you don't mind ...' He was perfectly well aware that Alexei knew where he was going – he had gone to the Armenia every Friday night for years past, but his detective captain gravely nodded as if he didn't know the boss was itching to get off on his night with the boys.

'I'll get over to the Metropol and bring this Smith in, then.' He spoke as if he hoped that Mitin would countermand the order even at this eleventh hour, but the commissioner merely waved him away with his blessing.

'A good day's work, Alexei Alexandrovich – we'll make a detective of you yet, before you retire!'

He waddled across the room to get his cap and Pudovkin retreated backwards to the door.

'I'd better tell the British Consul – and the Swiss one, I suppose.'

Mitin lumbered across the room, literally forcing Alexei through the door. 'Yes, you do that ... tell me all about it in the morning.'

Even Pudovkin's thick skin could hardly turn aside the impression that the interview was over, so he went downstairs to his office to collect Moiseyenko.

The lieutenant was waiting for him with a message.

'Lev Pomansky rang a few minutes ago.'

'He hasn't lost Smith again?!' asked an anguished Pudovkin. 'Not now!'

Vasily hastily reassured him. 'No, the opposite, in fact. He's gone to the Moskva Hotel in Marx Prospect, with the woman, the courier and the man Shaw. They left the Metropol about half an hour ago and now Pomansky says they're having a meal and some drinks in the restaurant of the Moskva.'

Pudovkin found his own finger straying to his ear and hastily snatched it down. 'We'd better wait until they come back to their own hotel before we collect him ... another hour won't make any difference, as long as we know where he is. I want to get them all together when I snatch Smith ... if there's any collusion, it may scare the partner into doing something rash.'

He paused. 'What's Lev doing now?'

'Hanging about the Moskva looking as inconspicuous as an ostrich in a chicken run, I expect!'

'He's got a good heart, Vasily ... it's just that his feet are too big and his brain is too small. Is he going to ring in when they leave?'

'He said he would.'

'Then we'll sit it out here – go and put the pot on the gas.'

In the gloom that settled over the main characters in the Metropol affair after dinner that night, an unexpected twinkle of life came from Michael Shaw.

'Let's have a walk over to the Hotel Moskva,' he suddenly announced, as they sat aimlessly around the cleared table. 'A writing pal o' mine from Cork stayed there and reckoned it beat this old mausoleum hollow.'

No one seemed in the least bit keen. Simon pointedly ignored him; he was too preoccupied wondering when Pudovkin was going to decide to arrest him – and wondering what the hell had happened to his best suit!

Elizabeth Treasure still carried traces of the desperate defiance that she had displayed to Simon when the saga of the smuggled fivers was played out that afternoon. Gilbert Bynge was perhaps the least troubled, though his tic remained bad and he seldom let an opportunity pass to wring his hands and wail about what 'Head Office' would be saying by now.

Shaw continued to nag about going off somewhere else for a drink, and eventually Gilbert gave in and agreed to join him. 'We'll have to have another bite to eat if we do, but it'll be a change.' He added his persuasions and, for the sake of peace, Simon and Liz agreed, mainly because they had nothing else to pass the evening.

The Moskva was within sight of the Metropol, just across Revolution Square on Marx Prospect. It was a far more modern building, being a great triple block with a colonnaded front, towering above the lower end of Gorky Street. It was well-known, not only for its more elegant atmosphere, but because its picture adorned the label of every bottle of Stolichnaya vodka!

They walked to it in three minutes and soon were sitting in the restaurant. Like the building, this was a far more modern place than their own dining room in the Metropol.

The atmosphere of the group seemed to have gained nothing by the change of air … they sat around in strained silence until the waiters finally arrived. Even when they had acquired something to drink, conversation was sporadic and banal until the alcohol seeped into their systems and at least made each other's company bearable.

155

Simon and Liz played a half-hearted game of footsie under the table again, and Gilbert, with his usual facility, found a girl acquaintance in the shape of an Intourist guide to talk to on the next table.

Shaw seemed content to sit and drink in silence most of the time. They felt obliged to order some food but, as they had just eaten, they merely picked at a salad and some soup.

To escape the ponderous atmosphere, Simon and Liz danced quite a few times; the usual succession of waltzes and quicksteps being leavened with some jive and even a twist or two in the racier climate of the Moskva.

Their mood gradually lightened and when they sat the next one out, Shaw's brooding presence seemed less forbidding to Simon. The Irishman had never indicated by such as a flicker of an eyelid that only a few hours ago he had been threatening Simon with exposure to the militia. Simon wasn't sure whether he would have risked doing it, but he had no intention of calling the bluff, if that was what it was.

Simon was pinning his hopes on the Security police jumping Shaw when he kept the alternative rendezvous with Pabst, next morning in Gorky Park. Whether the other man would promptly drag Simon in with him was a risk he was willing to take – he prayed that the whole story of Shaw killing Fragonard would satisfy the Soviets enough for them to disregard his little part in the plot.

Suddenly, Michael Shaw stuck his hairy arm across the table.

'What time is it, folks – I've bashed me watch against the door, it's on the blink. Falling to bits, in fact.'

Idly, Simon noticed that both hands had indeed fallen off and were lying loose inside the glass.

'There's a darned great clock over there,' said Gilbert helpfully. His Russian girl had gone back to her party and he was with them again.

The restaurant clock said nine fifty – they had been there an hour already and Simon was beginning to feel more at ease with the world. He flagged a passing waiter down from orbit and rashly ordered another flask of vodka and a beef stroganoff.

'My God, you'll burst, you pig – you've had one meal already!'

Liz was coming back on to form again and in spite of everything, the frustrated 'old Adam' in him began to speculate on prospects for the night ahead.

She had lost a lot of her up-stage manner these past few days – rubbed off by the ding-dong events since Helsinki. To Simon, she became more and more attractive, especially when his libido was not crushed by the worries of the trip.

The band started again and they danced again. His stroganoff arrived in the surprisingly short time of fifteen minutes and he savoured it while Gilbert took Liz out for the next daring foxtrot.

Shaw said nothing, but eyed Simon with supercilious amusement. It was apparent that his drunken state could be switched on and off at will, irrespective of how much he'd had to drink. He seemed obsessed by the time tonight. He looked at the clock with annoying regularity and even at the ruined face of his own watch now and then.

Eventually he spoke, but it was nothing dramatic. 'Must go to see a man about a dog!' he muttered and lurched up from the table. He made his way out, moving slowly. He wore a good suit, though it was crumpled and needed cleaning. He had succumbed to Western convention enough to wear a tie, though the loose knot was inches below his collar; as fully a third of the Russian patrons wore no tie at all, *he needn't have bothered*, thought Simon acidly.

Shaw made for the door, his big shoulders drooped. He didn't waver at all, but he gripped the backs of chairs to steady himself. Simon couldn't decide whether he really *was* drunk or playing some stunt.

If he could have seen around corners, he would have found out. As soon as Michael Shaw left the restaurant, he straightencd up and moved quickly and purposefully. He had no real need to play the drunk, but it was the role he had kept up while on this job and he automatically stuck to it whilst under the public gaze.

In the deserted corridor, he hurried down stairs to the underground cloakrooms. A clock on the wall said ten twenty exactly.

He went into the basement toilets and went to the row of cubicles. A few of the doors were shut with the 'Engaged' signs up and he tightened his lips in annoyance when he saw the last door on the left was also closed.

When he got to it, he was relieved to see that it was merely pulled shut and was not occupied. He slipped in and bolted the door. Jumping up on the seat, he fumbled his hand behind the cistern up on the wall.

For a moment, his fingers found nothing at all and he began to curse Simon Smith, whose trick with Fragonard's pistol had given him the idea for this hiding place.

Then he came across something sticking up from the gap between the tank and the tiled wall. He gripped the end of it and pulled up a leather strap, carrying a wristwatch of about the same size as his own. Looking at it with satisfaction, he saw that it also had the hands lying loose inside the glass.

He took off his own watch and dropped it into the space behind the tank, then buckled on the new one. A moment later, he was heading back to the restaurant. At the doors, he resumed his rolling slouch and went back to the table. Gilbert was again on the floor with Liz Treasure and he was left alone with Simon, who eyed him sourly.

'Kept your part of the bargain?' muttered the younger man.

Shaw nodded calmly 'I always do – no point in turning muck over if there's naught to be gained but a smell.'

Simon thought about this typically Irish proverb for a moment, then asked, 'Got that straight about tomorrow morning?'

The bearded man shrugged indifferently. 'Won't be needed now – the job is done, as a matter of fact.'

Simon felt a sudden pang of annoyance, partly because Shaw had so easily avoided the trap he had optimistically laid, but partly chagrin at the professional succeeding where an amateur had bodged it all up.

'Had it dropped in your lap!' he said bitterly. 'All I've got is the leftovers from the cost of the trip and a good chance of being arrested.'

Shaw looked at him contemptuously. 'If ye're hinting at a cut of the proceeds, you can go to hell – though I'll buy you a drink the next time I see you in London – which might be in about twenty years, if the Soviet bobbies nab you!'

'I'll shop you as well, if they do, don't worry!' snarled Simon under his breath. The end of the dance and the return of the other two put a stop to any more acrimony, especially as Shaw suddenly seemed to have tired of the Hotel Moskva.

'I'm for bed – early mornings like today play the diwil with me constitution.' He uncoiled himself from the chair and stood up. He shot a sneer across to Liz and Simon. 'Don't come because of me, though.'

Gilbert, having lost his female company, was ready to join him. Simon looked at Elizabeth and she returned the meaningful glance with a similar thought in her mind.

They strolled out of the hotel into the Moscow night. A solid stream of traffic met them as they tried to cross the wide expanse of Manezhnaya Square at the bottom of

159

Gorky Street. They gave up their idea of a stroll around the block, starting back to the Metropol by the shortest route.

They reached the gloomy entrance after only one delay – Liz insisted on gazing for a couple of minutes at the illuminated red stars rotating on the tips of the Kremlin spires.

Simon urged her up the steps and through the tall glass doors, eager to take up where Fragonard had interrupted the previous evening. Then, in the centre of the foyer, was the sight least wanted to see in all the world – a pair of blue uniformed figures, the taller one waiting with hands on hips.

Pudovkin stepped forward to meet them, his eagle-like face grim.

'I am sorry, I must ask you all to come into the bureau here – I have an unpleasant task to perform.'

Simon knew only too well what task would be.

Chapter Thirteen

'This concerns only one of you, but I wish to display to the other tourists all the main facts so that you can be witness to what I think is called "fair play" in your idiom.'

Pudovkin stood before them in his now familiar way, back hunched and head thrust out. They had moved into the deserted Intourist office, just off the foyer – a large room hung with dozens of travel posters and airline publicity displays. Simon thought ironically that it was likely to be a long time before he needed any travel facilities out of the Soviet Union. Although his mind told him that this was 'it' – the final denouement, the arrest and another Moscow spy trial – his heart refused to give up a tiny grain of hope that somehow the nightmare might pass.

Pudovkin did nothing to encourage this hope.

He waved them all to the easy chairs that were scattered about the room. As soon as they were uneasily settled, he took a pace forward leaving Moiseyenko hovering in the background and Lev Pomansky with his broad back to the door.

Alexei looked down at Simon.

'Mr Smith, I regret this very much, but I have my duty to do.' He fished in his breast pocket and took out a folded document. 'I have here an order for your detention on a charge of murder – that you killed Jules Honore Fragonard earlier today.'

Expected as they were, the actual words shocked Simon into numbness. Foolishly, all he could think of was that the British bit about 'anything you might say will be taken down …' was apparently not the vogue in Russia.

He cleared his mind with an effort and picked up again halfway through Pudovkin's solemn speech – '… additional evidence was obtained this afternoon which makes further delay unjustified.'

'Additional evidence!' – *that bastard Shaw has split on me after all*, he thought. *Right, then I'll do all I can to land him in it with me!*

He shot a furious glance at the Irishman, and was disconcerted to see him shake his head ever so slightly and make a definite shrug. Though Simon didn't trust him a fraction of an inch, he gave him the benefit of the doubt for the moment. It was a symptom of his shocked state of mind that he had not yet fully comprehended that he was being charged for a murder that the other man had committed and that everything he could do to incriminate Shaw was fair game – but the thought of simultaneously having to confess his implication in the tool steel business stayed his tongue for the moment.

Gilbert and Elizabeth were staring at him as if he had suddenly grown horns. He found his voice. 'What additional evidence? Whatever it is, it's untrue. I didn't kill that man and it is bound to be proved so eventually.'

Pudovkin stepped back and sat on the arm of a chair, so that he still had the psychological advantage of being above the accused man.

'You are entitled to know … you will have the benefit of a Soviet lawyer to assist you with your defence and these matters of evidence will be thoroughly gone into before the trial, if the Public Prosecutor decides to press the case against you – which, I must warn you, is almost inevitable.'

Pudovkin's English, rusty for some years, had improved enormously with the use it had had over the past day or so, but he still took a long time to come to the point.

'The new evidence is scientific – the All-Union Institute for Research in Forensic Medicine has produced definite proof that you were in close contact with the dead man. Fibres from the suit you were wearing last night were found on the front of his dressing gown. There is no other suit like that in the Soviet Union, Mr Smith.'

There was a pregnant silence, while everyone stared at the suit he now wore as if expecting it to burst into flames with the enormity of Pudovkin's disclosure.

Elizabeth's knuckles came up to her mouth, like a shot from the old silent movies. 'Oh, Simon, they must know,' she breathed.

Simon wasn't sure what she was talking about, but Pudovkin was on to her like a terrier pouncing on a rat.

'What was that, Mrs Treasure ... I think you have not told us the whole truth about last night – please do so now, for your sake and Mr Smith's.'

She stared back at him wide-eyed, her mouth hidden, then shook her head.

Simon sighed heavily 'Go on, Liz – tell them. This fibre business can't be dodged, so they know I was in there – doesn't alter the fact that I didn't kill him.'

He stressed the 'I' and threw an indecisive glance at Michael Shaw.

Pudovkin's eyes switched back and forth between them like a spectator at Wimbledon. 'Well, please?' he snapped.

Liz Treasure looked round-eyed at Simon and he nodded curtly. She swallowed and began to whisper her story.

'Speak louder, please, this will have to be written down later on, but I want to hear it all now,' commanded the detective captain.

Obediently, she raised her voice to a barely audible level.

'Fragonard — he came to Simon's ... Mr Smith's room after we left the restaurant.'

'You were there?'

'Yes.'

163

'At what time?'

'Eleven fifteen – eleven thirty. Something like that.' Her voice dropped again and Pudovkin made an impatient pantomime of cupping a hand to his ear.

'As early as that? Are you sure?'

She nodded.

'And how long did you stay there – or how long did Smith stay there?'

'Only a few minutes. I told you, Fragonard came and took him away to his room.'

Pudovkin considered this. He looked back at Moiseyenko and spoke rapidly in Russian. 'Couldn't have happened then – hours too soon.'

The lieutenant nodded. 'But the black eye and injured head – that fits.'

Pudovkin turned back to Elizabeth. 'This is the truth now?' he demanded.

'Of course.' Even through her nervousness, she sounded offended.

'And Smith did not come back to you later.'

She coloured up. 'Of course not! Look, I've told you all I know.'

He grunted. 'I should ask you why you did not tell us before, but it seems obvious.' His bright eyes swivelled to Simon.

'Now, you heard that. You are not going to deny it, as you gave Mrs Treasure permission to speak. You denied it earlier today – another fact to add to your list of perjuries. Now, what is your version of the affair, faced with these facts, eh?'

He managed to be direct without blustering, and triumphant without sneering.

Simon took a deep breath and jumped into the treacherous quicksands of confession. *Put a foot wrong and you're in it up to your neck*, he thought.

'I admit being in Fragonard's room at the time Mrs Treasure states,' he began in a flat, low voice. He stared at Pudovkin's pistol belt; the shining eyes were too unnerving. 'Fragonard came to my room where I was talking to Mrs Treasure and wanted to talk. It was inconvenient, so we went to his.'

The detective's face remained impassive. If he wondered about the nature of the 'inconvenience' he did not show it.

'What was the dead man wearing?'

'His suit – the same one he had on in the restaurant.' Simon sounded puzzled. 'I remember now, when we got to his room, he took off the jacket and put on a dressing gown over his shirt and trousers.'

Pudovkin looked around at Moiseyenko, who shrugged.

Liz and Gilbert were listening with rapt attention. Shaw looked bored.

'What happened in the room?' went on Alexei, remorselessly.

'Fragonard was a little drunk,' Simon threw this in for good measure, though it was quite untrue. 'We began to argue and he became abusive – he actually spat in my face!'

As this was true and the memory still rankled, he was able to put genuine feeling into his words.

'He struck me and I lost my temper and hit him in the eye after struggling with him … he tripped and fell back, hitting his head on the wall or the doorpost. He was unconscious for a moment, but began to recover quickly, so I left him – that's the last I saw of him, alive.'

The next question was inevitable, but Simon had had time to think up his storyline.

'What was this argument concerned with?'

'Mrs Treasure here …' Simon spoke diffidently, looking with assumed reluctance towards Liz, using the opportunity to give her the shadow of a wink. 'Fragonard

165

had been trying to force his attentions on her during the sea voyage – and I objected.'

He threw this in as a weak but better-than-none excuse.

Pudovkin's leathery face wrinkled into a frown. 'You mean that the small old man was interfering with your woman friend?'

Simon gritted his teeth. The paths of liars were undoubtedly stony.

'Interfering is perhaps too strong – he was, well … chasing her, inflicting his company on her when it was not welcome – you understand me.'

Simon found himself slipping into basic English for Pudovkin's benefit, as the strain of interrogating in a foreign tongue seemed to be telling on him.

Alexei bobbed his head slowly. 'And because of this he tried to murder you in Helsinki,' he asked sarcastically.

Simon, pale and drawn, sighed. 'I told you. That must have been some common thief.'

Alexei let it go. 'Why did Fragonard call on you and not the other way around – you were the one objecting to his behaviour – so you *say*?'

Simon literally shrugged this off. 'He was drunk.'

'And because of this, you struck the old man a violent blow, causing unconsciousness?'

He made it sound shameful, like stealing a blind man's pennies.

'Hitting his head was an accident – he began the violence,' defended Simon. 'All I did was punch him back – in the eye …'

For a second, he contemplated telling them about Fragonard pulling a gun on him as an added provocation. This could easily be proved by dipping into the cistern, but would raise all sorts of deep enquiries about Fragonard's motives for being armed in Russia, a topic to be avoided like the plague.

'And when did you leave the room of the deceased?'

'Straight away – I wasn't in there more than ten minutes. Must have been back in my own room by eleven thirty or just after.'

'And no doubt you maintain, still, that you did not go back during the night.'

'I certainly do – the next thing I heard was all that row at five thirty today. Mrs Treasure came to tell me about it.'

'You were not out of your room at three in the morning and you say you heard nothing,' stated Pudovkin in frank disbelief.

While Simon agreed vehemently, Moiseyenko whispered something in his superior's ear and the two of them had a muttered conversation in their own language.

Pudovkin returned to the attack. 'I think you are telling us only half the truth, Mr Smith. You went back to Fragonard's room in the early hours of this morning and killed him with a blow to the throat, did you not?'

'I did not,' retorted Simon stonily to this frontal attack.

'You struck him in the throat, killed him and threw his dead body from the window. Were you in the armed forces?'

Simon stared blankly at this twist in the accusation.

'The army … yes, like most men in my age group.'

'You saw fighting?'

'Yes – what of it?'

Was this going to be some political angle?

'And all your troops, like Soviet soldiers, receive training in physical combat?' This was more a statement than a query.

Simon saw the relevance at last. 'No, I wasn't taught that – only special assault troops learn unarmed combat.'

Pudovkin shrugged and left it. 'The matter will now be out of my hands – my remaining duty is only to take you into custody, I am afraid. The future will be dealt with by the Public Prosecutor.'

He rose to his feet and looked around at the rest of the party.

'The Prosecutor will also decide on who he requires as witnesses – has anyone else anything to add?'

Elizabeth gave a loud sniff and laid her hand consolingly on Simon's arm.

Gilbert looked shocked, his mouth twitched and his prominent Adam's apple bobbed up and down like a yo-yo. 'Terrible affair!' he gulped at last. 'Some ghastly mistake, old boy ... look, I'd better muster the Consul and Embassy, eh?'

He even forgot 'London Office' in his consternation, though that, no doubt, would come to haunt him before long. He hopped up, his lanky body as tall as Pudovkin.

'I'd better nip off to the phone and see if I can raise any one at the Consulate at this time of night.' He rapidly changed to Russian and began a quick-fire exchange with Pudovkin.

The militia officer handed him a passport and Gilbert sat down again to copy the passport and visa numbers into his diary.

Pudovkin's eyes strayed to the silent member of the group, Michael Shaw. 'And you ... have you anything to say?'

Michael shook his head slowly. He was in a 'delicate situation', as diplomats are wont to say. He had kept his mouth shut about hearing Simon in Fragonard's room and had not offered any more damning fabrications of his own. This was not from any friendly spirit, but to avoid his being precipitated into the affair by Simon.

He saw that it was bound to come sooner or later, once Smith had chance to weigh up the balance between confessing to his espionage role and being wrongly accused of murder. As soon as he saw that there was no escape from a life sentence for a murder he hadn't committed, he would undoubtedly split on Shaw.

So the bearded Irishman eyed Pudovkin with veiled wariness. The essence of this particular situation was time. As a professional freelance agent, ex-criminal and confidence trickster, he had been in as tight a spot as this before and got away with it. His recipe for survival was thorough pre-planning. If he could keep things off the boil until eight o'clock the following morning – even if it meant vanishing into the back streets of Moscow overnight – he was sitting pretty.

Before leaving Stockholm, he had arranged an expensive, but vital, link in his travel arrangements. Through a telephone call to a contact in Vienna, he had booked a seat on a MALÉV[7] flight from Moscow to Budapest, leaving at eight next day – he had estimated that two days in the Soviet capital would see the tool steel business finished for better or worse.

The flight was booked under a Czech name and he had a corresponding set of false papers. The passport and visa carried photographs of him before he grew his beard – a few minutes' work with scissors and a razor would see him through to Budapest, as the security arrangements between internal transit points in Eastern Europe were far less stringent than on the usual East-West frontiers.

From Budapest, it was child's play to a man of his experience to cross into Austria. The 'Iron Curtain', now very rusty and perforated, was more like a colander to people of his calibre, especially on the Hungarian border. He reckoned that by the day after tomorrow, he could be back in Paris for the big pay-off from his American sponsors – rivals to the outfit that had employed Kramer.

All these considerations clicked through his mind as he faced Pudovkin and the answer about what to say appeared in his brain like the printout from a computer.

---

[7]Hungarian National Airlines

'I've nothing to add at all, captain – I think there must be some great mistake here. Mr Smith is the victim of some terrible coincidence.'

His volubility was right out of character, but he reasoned that, by siding strongly with Smith, he had a better chance to confuse the issue in the man's mind, to give him a better chance of a getaway.

Pudovkin nodded abruptly and turned to face Simon again.

'Then we must go, Mr Smith. Lieutenant Moiseyenko will accompany you to your room to fetch your clothing and necessities like shaving materials.'

He stepped back and jerked his head at Vasily.

Simon looked around the faces, all of which became white blurs.

So this was the moment, then. *Arrest, a prison cell – then what?* His mind seized up completely. Like an automaton, he stood up and started to walk for the last time to the lift and the endless cavern of passages on the fourth floor. As he passed Liz Treasure, she stared at him as if he were already a ghost. *Never make you now, darling*, he thought, with a tinge of regret.

But the nightmare was not yet over.

Before Simon was halfway to the swing-doors, there was a tramp of feet outside. The panels flew apart with a crash and Pomansky had to step smartly aside to avoid being trampled by three burly men. They were almost identical, dressed in extra-long fawn raincoats and wide-brimmed felt hats.

They stopped a few paces inside the doors and looked around with grim faces. One of them walked up to Pudovkin and showed him a card embossed with the insignia of the Ministry of the Interior.

Alexei had already recognized him as an official from the Kalinin Street branch of the KGB, an office that dealt with some of the internal security matters of the capital city itself. The militia officer remembered him from behind-the-scenes activities in a famous trial three years before … his name was Odilov and he was a very hard nut indeed.

Odilov spoke rapidly to Pudovkin. Although everyone in the room except Elizabeth spoke Russian, none of them could pick up the words, not even Moiseyenko, who was torn between edging up to his chief to eavesdrop and looking after his prisoner, whom everyone seemed to have forgotten.

Pudovkin's eyebrows climbed higher up his forehead. 'But I've just arrested the fellow!' he exclaimed testily. These were the first words any of the others managed to catch.

Odilov turned around and faced the British contingent for the first time. Simon, his wits partly restored by the interruption, noticed his flat, Slavic face, which could have jumped straight from the unkind pen of any Western cartoonist portraying the typical Russian.

The man swept his small eyes mound the group and let them settle on Michael Shaw.

He stood motionless for a moment, his short legs sticking out like tree stumps from under his long mackintosh. The Chicago-style trilby was pulled well down over his eyes and if the situation hadn't been so tense, it would have looked like some send-up of a third rate spy thriller.

'Mr Shaw – I think you lost your watch in the Hotel Moskva.'

His voice was flat and expressionless – he still spoke in Russian.

Simon felt devastated by the anti-climax. *All this pantomime, just to return a bloody wristwatch, in the middle of me being carted off to life imprisonment*, he thought bitterly.

He was wrong.

Shaw's face reddened and he slowly rose to his feet, towering over the KGB man.

'I don't know what you're talking about,' he rumbled, deliberately speaking in English.

Odilov smiled forbearingly and repeated himself in English, with sarcastic clarity.

'Nonsense – here's my watch!' snapped Shaw, jerking up his sleeve.

Odilov slowly withdrew a hand from his side pocket and dangled another wristwatch by its strap. He held it high, almost under Shaw's nose.

'This one says 'Made in England' on the face ... I have no doubt that the one you are wearing will say "Made in the USSR".'

He slowly lowered the watch and gazed sadly at the face.

'A pity – the hands seem to be detached – I wonder if the hands on yours are loose, also. May I see?'

He held out a hand.

Shaw made no movement, but his eyes flickered a little beneath lowered lids, as if he was seeking a way of escape.

'Let me see it!' said Odilov, more sharply this time.

His two henchmen closed in slightly. Pudovkin, Vasily and Pomansky stared in fascination, Simon Smith now forgotten.

Michael Shaw stood immobile for a few more seconds, then, ever so slowly like a film running at half speed, undid the buckle of his watch strap. He handed it reluctantly to the security man.

Odilov put the other watch back in his pocket and with a quick movement, bent down and put Shaw's on the terrazzo floor. He raised his heel and brought it down on the glass with a crack that echoed like a pistol shot around the deathly still room. Then he bent down and picked up the shattered timepiece and shook it gently over his cupped hand.

A black metallic powder trickled out from the battered face.

Michael Shaw watched it as if it were his own lifeblood draining away.

Odilov smiled a thin smile.

'No, Mr Shaw, not tool steel … just ordinary iron filings. We do not bait our traps with the real goods!'

He threw the wrecked watch contemptuously at Shaw's feet.

Chapter Fourteen

Simon later managed to piece together his recollections of the frantic moments that followed.

He remembered Shaw stooping to pick up the broken watch. No one spoke a word as he walked past Odilov to stand in front of Pudovkin.

The next thing Simon knew was that the watch had been flung in his own face and Shaw was shouting 'That's the man you want!'

Looking back on it, it was obviously only a diversion. At this dramatic gesture, all eyes automatically turned back to Simon to see what his reaction would be – he *was* the original villain of the piece. In that split second, Michael Shaw had hurled himself at the swing-doors and was galloping down the steps into the foyer before either the militia or the KGB men realized what had happened.

There was a hue and a cry like something from an old Keystone Cops film. Moiseyenko and Pomansky were first out of the Bureau – the doors swung back behind them with a crash, impeding Pudovkin and the security men for a second or two. The British party – or what was left of it – straggled out after them, Simon's arrest overshadowed.

Shaw had bolted down the four or five steps from the Intourist Bureau to the foyer, turned sharp left and sped down more steps through the second set of tall glass doors that led to the street. He had only four or five yards lead on Moiseyenko, but, with his massive physique and long legs, he kept that lead over the lieutenant, the youngest and most athletic of his pursuers.

Shaw skidded left again when he gained the pavement and went hammering off down Sverdlov Square in the direction of the Kremlin. There were few people about and those that failed to get out of the way were bowled over like skittles. The Irishman thundered by the petrol station beyond the hotel and carried on past a small ornamental garden. Pomansky had already fallen behind Moiseyenko and was puffing along with the also-rans, though the younger of the KGB agents overtook them and was pulling level with Vasily. The pavement curved towards the right as it approached the Lenin Museum, but at the middle of the curve there was a broad pathway leading through the garden, ending at the glass front of the Sverdlov Square Metro station.

Shaw hurled himself around into the path, extending his lead over Moiseyenko with every gigantic stride.

But now, the loyal citizens of Moscow were taking a hand. A thin stream of people came in the opposite direction, out of the brightly lit entrance of the Metro.

Though most of them shied away from the flailing arms and legs of the fugitive, one youth was willing to 'have a go'.

Quick-witted and agile, he threw himself sideways away from Shaw, but stuck a leg out in front of the running man. Shaw went flying, catapulting over the boy and landing heavily in the low privet hedge lining the pathway. The young man wisely rolled clear but, in a fraction of a second, Moiseyenko and the first KGB man were upon Shaw before he could begin to get up.

Pudovkin and Pomansky panted up and added their weight to the writhing pile of limbs that was macerating part of the pride and joy of the Moscow City Parks Department.

By the time that Gilbert Bynge and Simon arrived, Shaw was on his feet, gripped firmly by both shoulders and wrists. Moiseyenko and Lev Pomansky had him; the

KGB men seemed reluctant to take part in mere police duties.

Odilov joined them in time to set out back to the hotel, everyone breathing heavily with the sudden exertion. Hardly a word had been spoken the whole time – events seemed to speak for themselves.

The usual miraculous appearance of a crowd took place, but melted away much faster than would have the case in a Western city – the apprehension of criminals was a thing of no civic interest, just as court cases were rarely reported in the newspapers.

The straggling group started off down the pathway, silent apart from heavy breathing and a grunted 'Come on, you!' from Pomansky.

Shaw, his chest heaving, walked reluctantly, his head bent down. The fight seemed to have gone out of him, but he was only foxing – the drama had yet to be completed.

As they drew level with the petrol pumps at the side of the Metropol, he gave a strangled yelp of pain, and stumbled against Moiseyenko.

'My ankle!' he gasped as his right foot twisted and his weight fell on Vasily's arm.

Almost as a reflex, the two militiamen let him free and looked down at the 'injured' leg.

Like greased lightning, Shaw was off again. His sheer bulk bulldozed Moiseyenko aside, who cannoned into Odilov, making him stumble in turn. The Irishman was across the pavement and into the road like a flash, but this time he had no chance. One of the security men pulled a heavy automatic from the raincoat pocket where he had been discreetly hiding it against just such an event. He fired at no more than ten feet range and hit Shaw in the thigh, just as he was running between two cars parked at the kerbside.

The heavy bullet seemed to jerk him bodily forwards, then he pitched full length into the open road.

Right under the front wheels of a red Likachev-built motor coach.

Alexei Pudovkin leaned back in his creaky old chair in Petrovka and lit his first Aurora of the day.

Moiseyenko was perched in his usual place on the edge of the desk.

'Think Shaw was telling the truth?'

Alexei nodded, screwing up his eyes against the smoke as he waved out a match. 'No point in him saying otherwise. He knew he was dying when we pulled him out from under that autobus – he only had a chance to say "I killed Chenier" before he passed out. That was enough for Odilov – Chenier was the name by which they knew Fragonard for some other espionage job across the Finnish border.'

'And the fingerprint clinched his involvement, anyway.'

A fragment of a fingerprint, found later on the edge of the trigger-guard of the Chylewski pistol from the ship, had matched one of those taken from Michael Shaw earlier on the day of his death.

'He'd wiped the gun before planting it on Smith to incriminate him for some reason,' said Pudovkin, 'but he'd missed that one tiny area.'

'So we'd have got him eventually,' reflected Vasily. 'Even if the crowd from The Centre hadn't beaten us to it.'

Alexei nodded and they both silently digested their thoughts for a moment.

'So we let him go!' Moiseyenko seemed regretful that Simon Smith was now on his way back across Europe instead of being inside Lubyanka.

Alexei gave one of his shrugs. 'The Prosecutor and the big noises "over the wall" got together, so I understand from Igor Mitin – they decided to tell the British Embassy that Smith would be allowed to leave as a gesture of goodwill between our countries and all that sort of stuff.'

'On conditions!' barked Vasily.

Alexei flickered his ash into the empty cigarette packet. 'Aye, our comrade Smith won't get a visa for the Soviet Union again – nor any of the other socialist states, if I know Odilov. He'll "blacklist" him from Berlin to Sofia.'

'He's too damned lucky, that Smith,' grumbled Moiseyenko, 'He was up to something on the *Yuri Dolgorukiy* or Shaw would never have planted that gun, nor attacked him in Helsinki – funny that, everyone, even Smith himself, thought it was Fragonard who threw him in the dock.'

Alexei puffed out some smoke toward the ceiling. 'He was up to something all right – but Fragonard and Shaw were the big fish. The Ministry of the Interior evidently think that, with both of *them* dead, it's not worth pushing a case against Smith; he must have been small fry.'

Moiseyenko scowled. 'We'll never know the whole truth – nor anything approaching it. Those fellows from Dzerzhinsky Street wouldn't tell their own grandmothers the day of the week!'

He was obviously fishing, and Alexei, feeling expansive under the soothing effect of nicotine, took pity on him.

'Odilov let fall a few tit-bits – grudgingly enough, but he remembered me from the time one of our militiamen got mixed up in a security job in Krasnogorsk a few years ago.'

He paused for another long pull at his Aurora. 'Both this Fragonard – or Chenier, if you like – and the man Shaw were after some tool steel. They were both agents for Western industrialists ... I don't know the details. I don't think Odilov does either, but he wouldn't admit it. Somehow, they got a German in the Likachev works to agree to smuggle some out. The KGB had wind of this a long while ago, but they wanted to catch him red-handed. They picked him up eventually, after following him to Gorky Park where he obviously had a rendezvous with someone. Odilov put a substitute there at once, but the contact never turned up, or was scared off – the German didn't know him, he'd never met any of the bunch in the Metropol. Odilov kept the substitute working in the factory and watched the flat and sure enough, there was an anonymous phone call. It must have been Shaw, of course – he fixed another rendezvous for handing the stuff over.'

Moiseyenko saw a flaw in this. 'Why would he risk ringing the man's home, if he had suspected a trap earlier in the day?'

Alexei grunted. 'I don't know – perhaps he just couldn't get to the rendezvous – or just took the risk.'

'Or it was a different person!' said Moiseyenko ominously, thinking of Smith safely trundling across Holland by now.

Pudovkin grinned at him and his transparent anger at Simon's escape.

'Anyway, the message arranged for a wristwatch filled with the stuff to be left behind a certain lavatory cistern in the Hotel Moskva at ten-fifteen that night' went on the detective captain, 'so the mob from The Centre obliged with a watch filled with iron filings.

They waited to see who collected it – Shaw of course – then followed him back here to arrest him. Now Odilov and his bosses are as mad as hell because they've been cheated out of a nice propaganda-rich trial!'

Vasily chewed his lip thoughtfully. 'Wonder where he was trying to escape to – Shaw, I mean? Running round the streets of Moscow is a pretty futile way of trying to get out of the USSR. The Embassy wouldn't have touched him with a bargepole, I'm sure.'

Alexei scraped his chair back and stood up. 'The instincts of the hunted, I suppose – run away and hide. It's almost an animal reflex.'

He took his hat off the filing cabinet. 'That's what I'm doing now – running away home, off to brave Darya in her den – wonder what mood she's in this evening!'

'It was a helluva sight easier to get in and out of Russia than it is to get back into Britain,' grumbled Simon, as he held Liz Treasure's arm in the queue.

The boat from the Hook of Holland had just arrived at Harwich, bringing on almost the last stage of the long train and boat journey from Moscow.

That forty-eight hours, including a night stop at West Berlin, had been long enough to eliminate most of the immediate effects of the last awful day in the Soviet capital. Now his mind was full of more attractive things, like the eight hundred pounds' profit he had made on Kramer's advance and, of course, the prospect of a London containing Elizabeth Treasure.

She had been at her most attractive on the overland journey. Once the train pulled out of the Byelorusskiy station, she progressively lost her fear of arrest. When Simon had been deported, the day following the deaths, she had at once volunteered to go with him, declaring that she had had enough of Russia. The rest of the Trans-Europa tour stayed on to finish their ten days, while Simon and Liz were quietly pushed out of the country. There were no immediate vacancies on air flights, and rather than wait in Moscow and risk a change of heart by the authorities, Simon offered to go by rail.

Liz still stuck to him and by the time the express had reached Brest-Litovsk to change its axles for the standard gauge beyond the Polish frontier, she was positively vivacious again.

181

The train was almost empty for the rest of its run from Terespol to Berlin and they made good use of the solitude, to the embarrassment of the little coach conductor.

They spent the next night together in a Berlin hotel, just off the Kurfürstendamm, and Elizabeth's spirits seemed to soar even higher next day as the train neared the Hook of Holland.

The boat did not run to a double cabin for them, but she seemed just as affectionate next morning. They stood now waiting in the Immigration bay and Simon had the frightening feeling that he was slipping into love with her.

He had never seen her look so attractive … it may have been his newly biased eyes, but she looked even lovelier than usual. The suit she wore was chic and flattering – he'd not seen it before. He wondered where she managed to pack all these clothes – *this one certainly didn't come out of a false bottom in the old brown case*, he thought! He looked her up and down again as they shuffled forward in the queue – she really was beautiful. More make-up than usual, perhaps, and that extra bit of grooming that managed to gild the lily even more than on other days – he wondered vainly if it was for his benefit; could this falling in love routine be mutual?

Fearful words like 'engagement' and even 'marriage' reared up in the back of his mind – things that he had spent years running from, yet today they didn't seem nearly so painful!

He struggled to hold her arm and carry her cases with the other. His own case was at his feet and he was shuffling it along with them as they moved.

Eventually, they arrived at the desks, where hardfaced officials glowered resentfully at the travellers.

With grudging suspicion, they finally allowed the Britons to set foot once more on their native soil.

After convincing a cold-eyed man that the photo in his passport really was that of Simon Smith, they moved into the Customs Hall and found a space at the low counters to settle their cases.

Elizabeth lifted her two smaller ones up alongside his, smiled sweetly at him and touched his arm with an elegantly gloved hand.

'Nearly home,' she murmured in his ear.

A Customs Officer approached, *dressed in the uniform of at least a Vice-Admiral*, thought Simon. He had never paid a penny in duty, yet automatically tensed himself for a battle of wits, in true British anti-Revenue tradition.

'Any gifts, sir?' after the cardboard list had been offered and read.

In spite of the cloud under which he had left the Metropol, Simon had managed a few minutes in the hotel shop.

'A fur hat, some caviar … a bottle of vodka … and, oh, a *matryoshka* for my little niece.'

The 'admiral' insisted on seeing the fur hat, but charged nothing on it.

Elizabeth had nothing at all to declare and the suspicious Excise man went through all her cases. Finding nothing – not even a false bottom on the return trip – he sulkily made a magic chalk mark on the sides of their bags and they moved through to the boat-train platform.

During the trip to Liverpool Street, Simon basked in Liz's company. Again he wondered at her special elegance and decided perhaps it was not all for him, but just a token of a safe return to her dear old London.

His mind wandered through various ways of setting some permanent seal on their holiday affair. A good dinner and a night on the town to celebrate his deliverance from Lubyanka seemed the first way of cutting in to Kramer's money.

When they reached Liverpool Street, he was all for hailing a taxi and rushing off for the most expensive lunch they could find, but she steered him into the cocktail lounge of the station hotel and demanded a gin and tonic.

'I cabled my friend to meet me here – the one who put up that money. You understand, dear, don't you ... you don't mind waiting a little?'

Simon minded like hell, but he saw that the loss of two hundred quid had to be explained away and the sooner the blow was delivered, the better.

Dumping the bags just inside the door, he settled Liz at a table and went for some drinks. When he came back, he found her rummaging around in the huge handbag she carried. She brought out a gaudily painted wooden doll, another *matryoshka* similar to Simon's present for his sister's child, only a little smaller. The dolls consisted of a nest of five or six, all one inside the other down to the tiny central figure.

He stared at it. 'I didn't know you had bought a set as well?'

She smiled sweetly at him.

'I didn't, darling – these are the inside bits of yours. I've been a bit naughty – I pinched it from your case when we were on the train in Russia.'

He felt a sinking feeling in the pit of his stomach.

'My God, Liz ... what the hell have you been up to now!'

He grabbed the doll from her and feverishly took it to bits, splitting the hollow shells right down to the one in the middle.

Thankfully, he found nothing – he half expected to find it stuffed with antique jewels bought with black market roubles.

'What about the outer one – where's that?'

She smiled again and held out scarlet-tipped fingers.

'You've got it, darling – can I see, please?'

Mystified and apprehensive, Simon reached down and snapped open his case and took out the big *matryoshka*.

The motherly-looking doll, with its painted red cheeks, smiled smugly at him as he placed it hesitantly on the low table between them.

Elizabeth calmly cracked it open and deftly took out the tightly rolled wad of five-pound notes that was crammed into the cavity.

'Got them all in, darling … you don't think I could have watched this lot go down the loo, surely – thanks for getting them in for me. You would have explained things far better than I, if they'd been found … ah, there's my friend!'

She slipped the fivers into her bag and quickly stood up.

'Bye-bye, darling – it was lovely fun while it lasted.'

She bent down and kissed him lightly on the forehead, then switched and trotted daintily across the lounge.

A dark-haired girl in a striking yellow dress stood alone in the centre of the room, but Simon watched aghast as Liz walked straight past her and went up to a tall man in an officer-pattern overcoat and a City bowler. She stood on tip-toe to kiss him warmly below his stylish moustache. Hugging his arm, she walked out of the lounge without a backward glance.

A porter came in and carted off her bags, but Simon didn't notice.

He sat numbed for a moment, looking at the *matryoshka*, then up at the empty doorway.

His gaze drifted back to the gutted doll on the table. It looked as empty as his soul felt at that moment.

'You're hollow,' he muttered at the little wooden figure. 'You're all bloody hollow! … damn all women!'

Alexei Pudovkin was in his stockinged feet again, slumped in his battered armchair, the one that Darya was always threatening to throw out.

His promised reconciliation had lasted thirty-six hours. Now, he was back to the high-pitched nagging, the crash of pots and pans and a holiday in the Crimea.

With the end of his great new case and the return of routine petty thefts and family assaults, his newly won dominance had wilted and with it went his mastery over his wife.

He gulped down his beer and poured another ... Vasily had been up here sharing it with him, but Darya had driven him away to drink in peace at the athletic club.

Alexei groaned as she flounced into the living room and whipped away the tablecloth with a flourish like a bullfighter.

'Going to sit there all evening, soaking yourself in drink? Can't you even watch television, like other men, instead of reading all those old police books!'

She stalked away and Alexei hurled his copy of the *Criminal Code of the USSR* into the corner of the room, in a slow build-up of rage.

Reaching out to his bookshelf, he took down the Civil *Code* instead and turned angrily to the section on 'Divorce'.

'Damn all women!' he snarled under his breath.

The Sixties Mysteries
by
Bernard Knight

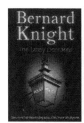  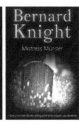 

The Lately Deceased
The Thread of Evidence
Mistress Murder
Russian Roulette
Policeman's Progress
Tiger at Bay
The Expert

For more information about **Bernard Knight**

and other **Accent Press** titles

please visit

www.accentpress.co.uk

15162107R00119

Printed in Poland
by Amazon Fulfillment
Poland Sp. z o.o., Wrocław